The "Goldfish"

Arthur Cheney Train

The "Goldfish"

ISBN: 978-1-64799-013-8

CONTENTS

CONTENTS

CHAPTER I

MYSELF

"My house, my affairs, my ache and my religion—"

I was fifty years old to-day. Half a century has hurried by since I first lay in my mother's wondering arms. To be sure, I am not old; but I can no longer deceive myself into believing that I am still young. After all, the illusion of youth is a mental habit consciously encouraged to defy and face down the reality of age. If, at twenty, one feels that he has reached man's estate he, nevertheless, tests his strength and abilities, his early successes or failures, by the temporary and fictitious standards of youth.

At thirty a professional man is younger than the business man of twenty-five. Less is expected of him; his work is less responsible; he has not been so long on his job. At forty the doctor or lawyer may still achieve an unexpected success. He has hardly won his spurs, though in his heart he well knows his own limitations. He can still say: "I am young yet!" And he is.

But at fifty! Ah, then he must face the facts! He either has or has not lived up to his expectations and he never can begin over again. A creature of physical and mental habit, he must for the rest of his life trudge along in the same path, eating the same food, thinking the same thoughts, seeking the same pleasures—until he acknowledges with grim reluctance that he is an old man.

I confess that I had so far deliberately tried to forget my approaching fiftieth milestone, or at least to dodge it with closed eyes as I passed it by, that my daughter's polite congratulation on my demicentennial anniversary gave me an unexpected and most unpleasant shock.

"You really ought to be ashamed of yourself!" she remarked as she joined me at breakfast.

"Why?" I asked, somewhat resenting being thus definitely proclaimed as having crossed into the valley of the shadows.

"To be so old and yet to look so young!" she answered, with charming voir-faire.

Then I knew the reason of my resentment against fate. It was because I was labeled as old while, in fact, I was still young. Of course that was it. Old? Ridiculous! When my daughter was gone I gazed searchingly at myself in the mirror. Old? Nonsense!

I saw a man with no wrinkles and only a few crow's-feet such

1

as anybody might have had; with hardly a gray hair on my temples and with not even a suggestion of a bald spot. My complexion and color were good and denoted vigorous health; my flesh was firm and hard on my cheeks; my teeth were sound, even and white; and my eyes were clear save for a slight cloudiness round the iris.

The only physical defect to which I was frankly willing to plead guilty was a flabbiness of the neck under the chin, which might by a hostile eye have been regarded as slightly double. For the rest I was strong and fairly well—not much inclined to exercise, to be sure, but able, if occasion offered, to wield a tennis racket or a driver with a vigor and accuracy that placed me well out of the duffer class.

Yes; I flattered myself that I looked like a boy of thirty, and I felt like one—except for things to be hereinafter noted—and yet middle-aged men called me "sir" and waited for me to sit down before doing so themselves; and my contemporaries were accustomed to inquire jocularly after my arteries. I was fifty! Another similar stretch of time and there would be no I. Twenty years more—with ten years of physical effectiveness if I were lucky! Thirty, and I would be useless to everybody. Forty—I shuddered. Fifty, I would not be there. My room would be vacant. Another face would be looking into the mirror.

Unexpectedly on this legitimate festival of my birth a profound melancholy began to possess my spirit. I had lived. I had succeeded in the eyes of my fellows and of the general public. I was married to a charming woman. I had two marriageable daughters and a son who had already entered on his career as a lawyer. I was prosperous. I had amassed more than a comfortable fortune. And yet—

These things had all come, with a moderate amount of striving, as a matter of course. Without them, undoubtedly I should be miserable; but with them—with reputation, money, comfort, affection—was I really happy? I was obliged to confess I was not. Some remark in Charles Reade's Christie Johnstone came into my mind—not accurately, for I find that I can no longer remember literally—to the effect that the only happy man is he who, having from nothing achieved money, fame and power, dies before discovering that they were not worth striving for.

I put to myself the question: Were they worth striving for? Really, I did not seem to be getting much satisfaction out of them. I began to be worried. Was not this an attitude of age? Was I not an old man, perhaps, regardless of my youthful face?

At any rate, it occurred to me sharply, as I had but a few more years of effective life, did it not behoove me to pause and see, if I

2

could, in what direction I was going?—to "stop, look and listen"?—to take account of stock?—to form an idea of just what I was worth physically, mentally and morally?—to compute my assets and liabilities?—to find out for myself by a calm and dispassionate examination whether or not I was spiritually a bankrupt? That was the hideous thought which like a deathmask suddenly leered at me from behind the arras of my mind—that I counted for nothing—cared really for nothing! That when I died I should have been but a hole in the water!

The previous evening I had taken my two distinctly blasé daughters to see a popular melodrama. The great audience that packed the theater to the roof went wild, and my young ladies, infected in spite of themselves with the same enthusiasm, gave evidences of a quite ordinary variety of excitement; but I felt no thrill. To me the heroine was but a painted dummy mechanically repeating the lines that some Jew had written for her as he puffed a reeking cigar in his rear office, and the villain but a popinjay with a black whisker stuck on with a bit of pitch. Yet I grinned and clapped to deceive them, and agreed that it was the most inspiriting performance I had seen in years.

In the last act there was a horserace cleverly devised to produce a convincing impression of reality. A rear section of the stage was made to revolve from left to right at such a rate that the horses were obliged to gallop at their utmost speed in order to avoid being swept behind the scenes. To enhance the realistic effect the scenery itself was made to move in the same direction. Thus, amid a whirlwind of excitement and the wild banging of the orchestra, the scenery flew by, and the horses, neck and neck, raced across the stage—without progressing a single foot.

And the thought came to me as I watched them that, after all, this horserace was very much like the life we all of us were living here in the city. The scenery was rushing by, time was flying, the band was playing—while we, like the animals on the stage, were in a breathless struggle to attain some goal to which we never got any nearer.

Now as I smoked my cigarette after breakfast I asked myself what I had to show for my fifty years. What goal or goals had I attained? Had anything happened except that the scenery had gone by? What would be the result should I stop and go with the scenery? Was the race profiting me anything? Had it profited anything to me or anybody else? And how far was I typical of a class?

A moment's thought convinced me that I was the prototype of thousands all over the United States. "A certain rich man!" That was me. I had yawned for years at dozens of sermons about men exactly

3

like myself. I had called them twaddle. I had rather resented them. I was not a sinner—that is, I was not a sinner in the ordinary sense at all. I was a good man—a very good man. I kept all the commandments and I acted in accordance with the requirements of every standard laid down by other men exactly like myself. Between us, I now suddenly saw, we made the law and the prophets. We were all judging ourselves by self-made tests. I was just like all the rest. What was true of me was true of them.

And what were we, the crowning achievement of American civilization, like? I had not thought of it before. Here, then, was a question the answer to which might benefit others as well as myself. I resolved to answer it if I could—to write down in plain words and cold figures a truthful statement of what I was and what they were.

I had been a fairly wide reader in my youth, and yet I did not recall anywhere precisely this sort of self-analysis. Confessions, so called, were usually amatory episodes in the lives of the authors, highly spiced and colored by emotions often not felt at the time, but rather inspired by memory. Other analyses were the contented, narratives of supposedly poverty-stricken people who pretended they had no desires in the world save to milk the cows and watch the grass grow. "Adventures in contentment" interested me no more than adventures in unbridled passion.

I was going to try and see myself as I was—naked. To be of the slightest value, everything I set down must be absolutely accurate and the result of faithful observation. I believed I was a good observer. I had heard myself described as a "cold proposition," and coldness was a sine qua non of my enterprise. I must brief my case as if I were an attorney in an action at law. Or rather, I must make an analytical statement of fact like that which usually prefaces a judicial opinion. I must not act as a pleader, but first as a keen and truthful witness and then as an impartial judge. And at the end I must either declare myself innocent or guilty of a breach of trust— pronounce myself a faithful or an unworthy servant.

I must dispassionately examine and set forth the actual conditions of my home life, my business career, my social pleasures, the motives animating myself, my family, my professional associates, and my friends—weigh our comparative influence for good or evil on the community and diagnose the general mental, moral and physical condition of the class to which I belonged.

To do this aright, I must see clearly things as they were without regard to popular approval or prejudice, and must not hesitate to call them by their right names. I must spare neither myself nor anybody else. It would not be altogether pleasant. The disclosures of the microscope are often more terrifying than the

4

amputations of the knife; but by thus studying both myself and my contemporaries I might perhaps arrive at the solution of the problem that was troubling me—that is to say, why I, with every ostensible reason in the world for being happy, was not! This, then, was to be my task.

* * * * *

I have already indicated that I am a sound, moderately healthy, vigorous man, with a slight tendency to run to fat. I am five feet ten inches tall, weigh a hundred and sixty-two pounds, have gray eyes, a rather aquiline nose, and a close-clipped dark-brown mustache, with enough gray hairs in it to give it dignity. My movements are quick; I walk with a spring. I usually sleep, except when worried over business. I do not wear glasses and I have no organic trouble of which I am aware. The New York Life Insurance Company has just reinsured me after a thorough physical examination. My appetite for food is not particularly good, and my other appetites, in spite of my vigor, are by no means keen. Eating is about the most active pleasure that I can experience; but in order to enjoy my dinner I have to drink a cocktail, and my doctor says that is very bad for my health.

My personal habits are careful, regular and somewhat luxurious. I bathe always once and generally twice a day. Incidentally I am accustomed to scatter a spoonful of scented powder in the water for the sake of the odor. I like hot baths and spend a good deal of time in the Turkish bath at my club. After steaming myself for half an hour and taking a cold plunge, an alcohol rub and a cocktail, I feel younger than ever; but the sight of my fellow men in the bath revolts me. Almost without exception they have flabby, pendulous stomachs out of all proportion to the rest of their bodies. Most of them are bald and their feet are excessively ugly, so that, as they lie stretched out on glass slabs to be rubbed down with salt and scrubbed, they appear to be deformed. I speak now of the men of my age. Sometimes a boy comes in that looks like a Greek god; but generally the boys are as weird-looking as the men. I am rambling, however. Anyhow I am less repulsive than most of them. Yet, unless the human race has steadily deteriorated, I am surprised that the Creator was not discouraged after his first attempt.

I clothe my body in the choicest apparel that my purse can buy, but am careful to avoid the expressions of fancy against which Polonius warns us. My coats and trousers are made in London, and so are my underclothes, which are woven to order of silk and cotton. My shoes cost me fourteen dollars a pair; my silk socks, six dollars; my ordinary shirts, five dollars; and my dress shirts, fifteen dollars each. On brisk evenings I wear to dinner and the opera a mink-lined overcoat, for which my wife recently paid seven hundred and fifty dollars. The storage and insurance on this coat come to twenty-five dollars annually and the repairs to about forty-five. I am rather fond of overcoats and own half a dozen of them, all made in Inverness.

I wear silk pajamas—pearl-gray, pink, buff and blue, with frogs, cuffs and monograms—which by the set cost me forty dollars. I also have a pair of pearl evening studs to wear with my dress suit, for which my wife paid five hundred and fifty dollars, and my cuff buttons cost me a hundred and seventy-five. Thus, if I am not an exquisite—which I distinctly am not—I am exceedingly well dressed, and I am glad to be so. If I did not have a fur coat to wear to the opera I should feel embarrassed, out of place and shabby. All the men who sit in the boxes at the Metropolitan Opera House have fur overcoats.

As a boy I had very few clothes indeed, and those I had were made to last a long time. But now without fine raiment I am sure I should be miserable. I cannot imagine myself shabby. Yet I can imagine any one of my friends being shabby without feeling any uneasiness about it—that is to say, I am the first to profess a democracy of spirit in which clothes cut no figure at all. I assert that it is the man, and not his clothes, that I value; but in my own case my silk-and-cotton undershirt is a necessity, and if deprived of it I should, I know, lose some attribute of self.

At any rate, my bluff, easy, confident manner among my fellow men, which has played so important a part in my success, would be impossible. I could never patronize anybody if my necktie were frayed or my sleeves too short. I know that my clothes are as much a part of my entity as my hair, eyes and voice—more than any of the rest of me.

Based on the figures given above I am worth—the material part of me—as I step out of my front door to go forth to dinner, something over fifteen hundred dollars. If I were killed in a railroad accident all these things would be packed carefully in a box, inventoried, and given a much greater degree of attention than my mere body. I saw Napoleon's boots and waistcoat the other day in Paris and I felt that he himself must be there in the glass case beside me.

Any one who at Abbotsford has felt of the white beaver hat of Sir Walter Scott knows that he has touched part—and a very considerable part—of Sir Walter. The hat, the boots, the waistcoat

6

are far less ephemeral than the body they protect, and indicate almost as much of the wearer's character as his hands and face. So I am not ashamed of my silk pajamas or of the geranium powder I throw in my bath. They are part of me.

But is this "me" limited to my body and my clothes? I drink a cup of coffee or a cocktail: after they are consumed they are part of me; are they not part of me as I hold the cup or the glass in my hand? Is my coat more characteristic of me than my house—my sleeve-links than my wife or my collie dog? I know a gentlewoman whose sensitive, quivering, aristocratic nature is expressed far more in the Russian wolfhound that shrinks always beside her than in the aloof, though charming, expression of her face. No; not only my body and my personal effects but everything that is mine is part of me—my chair with the rubbed arm; my book, with its marked pages; my office; my bank account, and in some measure my friend himself.

Let us agree that in the widest sense all that I have, feel or think is part of me—either of my physical or mental being; for surely my thoughts are more so than the books that suggest them, and my sensations of pleasure or satisfaction equally so with the dinner I have eaten or the cigar I have smoked. My ego is the sum total of all these things. And if the cigar is consumed, the dinner digested, the pleasure flown, the thought forgotten, the waistcoat or shirt discarded—so, too, do the tissues of the body dissolve, disintegrate and change. I can no more retain permanently the physical elements of my personality than I can the mental or spiritual.

What, then, am I—who, the Scriptures assert, am made in the image of God? Who and what is this being that has gradually been evolved during fifty years of life and which I call Myself? For whom my father and my mother, their fathers and mothers, and all my ancestors back through the gray mists of the forgotten past, struggled, starved, labored, suffered, and at last died. To what end did they do these things? To produce me? God forbid!

Would the vision of me as I am to-day have inspired my grandfather to undergo, as cheerfully as he did, the privations and austerities of his long and arduous service as a country clergyman— or my father to die at the head of his regiment at Little Round Top? What am I—what have I ever done, now that I come to think of it, to deserve those sacrifices? Have I ever even inconvenienced myself for others in any way? Have I ever repaid this debt? Have I in turn advanced the flag that they and hundreds of thousands of others, equally unselfish, carried forward?

Have I ever considered my obligation to those who by their patient labors in the field of scientific discovery have contributed

7

toward my well-being and the very continuance of my life? Or have I been content for all these years to reap where I have not sown? To accept, as a matter of course and as my due, the benefits others gave years of labor to secure for me? It is easy enough for me to say: No— that I have thought of them and am grateful to them. Perhaps I am, in a vague fashion. But has whatever feeling of obligation I may possess been evidenced in my conduct toward my fellows?

I am proud of my father's heroic death at Gettysburg; in fact I am a member, by virtue of his rank in the Union Army, of what is called The Loyal Legion. But have I ever fully considered that he died for me? Have I been loyal to him? Would he be proud or otherwise—is he proud or otherwise of me, his son? That is a question I can only answer after I have ascertained just what I am.

Now for over quarter of a century I have worked hard— harder, I believe, than most men. From a child I was ambitious. As a boy, people would point to me and say that I would get ahead. Well, I have got ahead. Back in the town where I was born I am spoken of as a "big man." Old men and women stop me on the main street and murmur: "If only your father could see you now!" They all seem tremendously proud of me and feel confident that if he could see me he would be happy for evermore. And I know they are quite honest about it all. For they assume in their simple hearts that my success is a real success. Yet I have no such assurance about it.

Every year I go back and address the graduating class in the high school—the high school I attended as a boy. And I am "Exhibit A"—the tangible personification of all that the fathers and mothers hope their children will become. It is the same way with the Faculty of my college. They have given me an honorary degree and I have given them a drinking fountain for the campus. We are a mutual-admiration society.

I am always picked by my classmates to preside at our reunions, for I am the conspicuous, shining example of success among them. They are proud of me, without envy. "Well, old man," they say, "you've certainly made a name for yourself!" They take it for granted that, because I have made money and they read my wife's name in the society columns of the New York papers, I must be completely satisfied.

And in a way I am satisfied with having achieved that material success which argues the possession of brains and industry; but the encomiums of the high-school principal and the congratulations of my college mates, sincere and well-meaning as they are, no longer quicken my blood; for I know that they are based on a total ignorance of the person they seek to honor. They see a heavily built, well-groomed, shrewd-looking man, with clear-cut features, a ready smile, and a sort of brusque frankness that seems to them the index of an honest heart. They hear him speak in a straightforward, direct way about the "Old Home," and the "Dear Old College," and "All Our Friends"—quite touching at times, I assure you—and they nod and say, "Good fellow, this! No frills—straight from the heart! No wonder he has got on in the city! Sterling chap! Hurrah!"

Perhaps, after all, the best part of me comes out on these occasions. But it is not the me that I have worked for half a century to build up; it is rather what is left of the me that knelt at my mother's side forty years ago. Yet I have no doubt that, should these good parents of mine see how I live in New York, they would only be the more convinced of the greatness of my success—the success to achieve which I have given the unremitting toil of thirty years.

* * * * *

And as I now clearly see that the results of this striving and the objects of my ambition have been largely, if not entirely, material, I shall take the space to set forth in full detail just what this material success amounts to, in order that I may the better determine whether it has been worth struggling for. Not only are the figures that follow accurate and honest, but I am inclined to believe that they represent the very minimum of expenditure in the class of New York families to which mine belongs. They may at first sight seem extravagant; but if the reader takes the trouble to verify them—as I have done, alas! many times to my own dismay and discouragement—he will find them economically sound. This, then, is the catalogue of my success.

I possess securities worth about seven hundred and fifty thousand dollars and I earn at my profession from thirty to forty thousand dollars a year. This gives me an annual income of from sixty-five thousand to seventy-five thousand dollars. In addition I own a house on the sunny side of an uptown cross street near Central Park which cost me, fifteen years ago, one hundred and twenty thousand dollars, and is now worth two hundred and fifty thousand. I could sell it for that. The taxes alone amount to thirty-two hundred dollars—the repairs and annual improvements to about twenty-five hundred. As the interest on the value of the property would be twelve thousand five hundred dollars it will be seen that merely to have a roof over my head costs me annually over eighteen thousand dollars.

My electric-light bills are over one hundred dollars a month. My coal and wood cost me even more, for I have two furnaces to heat the house, an engine to pump the water, and a second range in the laundry. One man is kept busy all the time attending to these matters and cleaning the windows. I pay my butler eighty dollars a month; my second man fifty-five; my valet sixty; my cook seventy; the two kitchen maids twenty-five each; the head laundress forty-five; the two second laundresses thirty-five each; the parlor maid thirty; the two housemaids twenty-five each; my wife's maid thirty-five; my daughter's maid thirty; the useful man fifty; the pantry maid twenty-five. My house payroll is, therefore, six hundred and fifty dollars a month, or seventy-eight hundred a year.

We could not possibly get along without every one of these servants. To discharge one of them would mean that the work would have to be done in some other way at a vastly greater expense. Add this to the yearly sum represented by the house itself, together with the cost of heating and lighting, and you have twenty-eight thousand four hundred dollars.

Unforeseen extras make this, in fact, nearer thirty thousand dollars. There is usually some alteration under way, a partition to be taken out, a hall to be paneled, a parquet floor to be relaid, a new sort of heating apparatus to be installed, and always plumbing. Generally, also, at least one room has to be done over and refurnished every year, and this is an expensive matter. The guest room, recently refurnished in this way at my daughter's request, cost thirty-seven hundred dollars. Since we average not more than two guests for a single night annually, their visits from one point of view will cost me this year eighteen hundred and fifty dollars apiece.

Then, too, styles change. There is always new furniture, new carpets, new hangings—pictures to be bought. Last season my wife changed the drawing room from Empire to Louis Seize at a very considerable outlay.

Our food, largely on account of the number of our servants, costs us from a thousand to twelve hundred dollars a month. In the spring and autumn it is a trifle less—in winter it is frequently more; but it averages, with wine, cigars, ice, spring water and sundries, over fifteen thousand dollars a year.

We rent a house at the seashore or in the country in summer at from five to eight thousand dollars, and usually find it necessary to employ a couple of men about the place.

Our three saddle-horses cost us about two thousand dollars for stabling, shoeing and incidentals; but they save me at least that in doctors' bills.

Since my wife and daughters are fond of society, and have different friends and different nightly engagements, we are forced to keep two motors and two chauffeurs, one of them exclusively for night-work. I pay these men one hundred and twenty-five dollars each a month, and the garage bill is usually two hundred and fifty more, not counting tires. At least one car has to be overhauled every year at an average expense of from two hundred and fifty to five hundred dollars. Both cars have to be painted annually. My motor service winter and summer costs on a conservative estimate at least eight thousand dollars.

I allow my wife five thousand dollars; my daughters three thousand each; and my son, who is not entirely independent, twenty-five hundred. This is supposed to cover everything; but it does not—it barely covers their bodies. I myself expend, having no vices, only about twenty-five hundred dollars.

The bills of our family doctor, the specialists and the dentist are never less than a thousand dollars, and that is a minimum. They would probably average more than double that.

Our spring trip to Paris, for rest and clothing, has never cost me less than thirty-five hundred dollars, and when it comes to less than five thousand it is inevitably a matter of mutual congratulation.

Our special entertaining, our opera box, the theater and social frivolities aggregate no inconsiderable sum, which I will not overestimate at thirty-five hundred dollars.

Our miscellaneous subscriptions to charity and the like come to about fifteen hundred dollars.

The expenses already recited total nearly seventy-five thousand dollars, or as much as my maximum income. And this annual budget contains no allowance for insurance, books, losses at cards, transportation, sundries, the purchase of new furniture, horses, automobiles, or for any of that class of expenditure usually referred to as "principal" or "plant." I inevitably am obliged to purchase a new motor every two or three years—usually for about six thousand dollars; and, as I have said, the furnishing of our city house is never completed.

It is a fact that for the last ten years I have found it an absolute impossibility to get along on seventy-five thousand dollars a year, even living without apparent extravagance. I do not run a yacht or keep hunters or polo ponies. My wife does not appear to be particularly lavish and continually complains of the insufficiency of her allowance. Our table is not Lucullan, by any means; and we rarely have game out of season, hothouse fruit or many flowers. Indeed, there is an elaborate fiction maintained by my wife, cook and butler that our establishment is run economically and strictly on a business basis. Perhaps it is. I hope so. I do not know anything

11

about it. Anyhow, here is the smallest budget on which I can possibly maintain my household of five adults:

ANNUAL BUDGET—MINIMUM—FOR FAMILY OF FIVE PERSONS

Taxes on city house $ 3,200
Repairs, improvements and minor alterations 2,500
Rent of country house—average 7,000
Gardeners and stablemen, and so on 800
Servants' payroll 7,800
Food supplies 15,000
Light and heat—gas, electricity, coal and wood 2,400
Saddle-horses—board and so on 2,000
Automobile expenses 8,000
Wife's allowance—emphatically insufficient 5,000
Daughters' allowance—two 6,000
Son's allowance 2,500
Self—clubs, clothes, and so on 2,500
Medical attendance—including dentist 1,000
Charity 1,500
Travel—wife's annual spring trip to Paris 3,500
Opera, theater, music, entertaining at restaurants,
and so on 3,500
_____

Total $74,200

A fortune in itself, you may say! Yet judged by the standards of expenditure among even the unostentatiously wealthy in New York it is moderate indeed. A friend of mine who has only recently married glanced over my schedule and said, "Why, it's ridiculous, old man! No one could live in New York on any such sum."

Any attempt to "keep house" in the old-fashioned meaning of the phrase would result in domestic disruption. No cook who was not allowed to do the ordering would stay with us. It is hopeless to try to save money in our domestic arrangements. I have endeavored to do so once or twice and repented of my rashness. One cannot live in the city without motors, and there is no object in living at all if

12

one cannot keep up a scale of living that means comfort and lack of worry in one's household.

The result is that I am always pressed for money even on an income of seventy-five thousand dollars. And every year I draw a little on my capital. Sometimes a lucky stroke on the market or an unexpected fee evens things up or sets me a little ahead; but usually January first sees me selling a few bonds to meet an annual deficit. Needless to say, I pay no personal taxes. If I did I might as well give up the struggle at once. When I write it all down in cold words I confess it seems ridiculous. Yet my family could not be happy living in any other way.

It may be remarked that the item for charity on the preceding schedule is somewhat disproportionate to the amount of the total expenditure. I offer no excuse or justification for this. I am engaged in an honest exposition of fact—for my own personal satisfaction and profit, and for what lessons others may be able to draw from it. My charities are negligible.

The only explanation which suggests itself to my mind is that I lead so circumscribed and guarded a life that these matters do not obtrude themselves on me. I am not brought into contact with the maimed, the halt and the blind; if I were I should probably behave toward them like a gentleman. The people I am thrown with are all sleek and well fed; but even among those of my friends who make a fad of charity I have never observed any disposition to deprive themselves of luxuries for the sake of others.

Outside of the really poor, is there such a thing as genuine charity among us? The church certainly does not demand anything approximating self-sacrifice. A few dollars will suffice for any appeal. I am not a professing Christian, but the church regards me tolerantly and takes my money when it can get it. But how little it gets! I give frequently—almost constantly—but in most instances my giving is less an act of benevolence than the payment of a tax upon my social standing. I am compelled to give. If I could not be relied upon to take tickets to charity entertainments and to add my name to the subscription lists for hospitals and relief funds I should lose my caste. One cannot be too cold a proposition. I give to these things grudgingly and because I cannot avoid it.

Of course the aggregate amount thus disposed of is really not large and I never feel the loss of it. Frankly, people of my class rarely inconvenience themselves for the sake of anybody, whether their own immediate friends or the sick, suffering and sorrowful. It is trite to say that the clerk earning one thousand dollars deprives himself of more in giving away fifty than the man with an income of twenty thousand dollars in giving away five thousand. It really costs the clerk more to go down into his pocket for that sum than the rich man to draw his check for those thousands.

Where there is necessity for generous and immediate relief I occasionally, but very rarely, contribute two hundred and fifty or five hundred dollars. My donation is always known and usually is noticed with others of like amount in the daily papers. I am glad to give the money and I have a sensation of making a substantial sacrifice in doing so. Obviously, however, it has cost me really nothing! I spend two hundred and fifty dollars or more every week or so on an evening's entertainment for fifteen or twenty of my friends and think nothing of it. It is part of my manner of living, and my manner of living is an advertisement of my success—and advertising in various subtle ways is a business necessity. Yet if I give two hundred and fifty dollars to a relief fund I have an inflation of the heart and feel conscious of my generosity.

I can frankly say, therefore, that so far as I am concerned my response to the ordinary appeal for charity is purely perfunctory and largely, if not entirely, dictated by policy; and the sum total of my charities on an income of seventy-five thousand dollars a year is probably less than fifteen hundred dollars, or about two per cent.

Yet, thinking it over dispassionately, I do not conclude from this that I am an exceptionally selfish man. I believe I represent the average in this respect. I always respond to minor calls in a way that pleases the recipient and causes a genuine flow of satisfaction in my own breast. I toss away nickels, dimes and quarters with prodigality; and if one of the office boys feels out of sorts I send him off for a week's vacation on full pay. I make small loans to seedy fellows who have known better days and I treat the servants handsomely at Christmas.

I once sent a boy to college—that is, I promised him fifty dollars a year. He died in his junior term, however. Sisters of Mercy, the postman, a beggar selling pencils or shoelaces—almost anybody, in short, that actually comes within range—can pretty surely count on something from me. But I confess I never go out of my way to look for people in need of help. I have not the time.

Several of the items in my budget, however, are absurdly low, for the opera-box which, as it is, we share with several friends and which is ours but once in two weeks, alone costs us twelve hundred dollars; and my bill at the Ritz—where we usually dine before going to the theater or sup afterward—is apt to be not less than one hundred dollars a month. Besides, twenty-five hundred dollars does not begin to cover my actual personal expenses; but as I am accustomed to draw checks against my office account and thrust the money in my pocket, it is difficult to say just what I do cost myself.

14

Moreover, a New York family like mine would have to keep surprisingly well in order to get along with but two thousand dollars a year for doctors. Even our dentist bills are often more than that. We do not go to the most fashionable operators either. There does not seem to be any particular way of finding out who the good ones are except by experiment. I go to a comparatively cheap one. Last month he looked me over, put in two tiny fillings, cleansed my teeth and treated my gums. He only required my presence once for half an hour, once for twenty minutes, and twice for ten minutes—on the last two occasions he filched the time from the occupant of his other chair. My bill was forty-two dollars. As he claims to charge a maximum rate of ten dollars an hour—which is about the rate for ordinary legal services—I have spent several hundred dollars' worth of my own time trying to figure it all out. But this is nothing to the expense incident to the straightening of children's teeth.

When I was a child teeth seemed to take care of themselves, but my boy and girls were all obliged to spend several years with their small mouths full of plates, wires and elastic bands. In each case the cost was from eighteen hundred to two thousand dollars. A friend of mine with a large family was compelled to lay out during the tooth-growing period of his offspring over five thousand dollars a year for several years. Their teeth are not straight at that.

Then, semioccasionally, weird cures arise and seize hold of the female imagination and send our wives and daughters scurrying to the parlors of fashionable specialists, who prescribe long periods of rest at expensive hotels—a room in one's own house will not do—and strange diets of mush and hot water, with periodical search parties, lighted by electricity, through the alimentary canal.

One distinguished medico's discovery of the terra incognita of the stomach has netted him, I am sure, a princely fortune. There seems to be something peculiarly fascinating about the human interior. One of our acquaintances became so interested in hers that she issued engraved invitations for a fashionable party at which her pet doctor delivered a lecture on the gastro-intestinal tract. All this comes high, and I have not ventured to include the cost of such extravagances in my budget, though my wife has taken cures six times in the last ten years, either at home or abroad.

And who can prophesy the cost of the annual spring jaunt to Europe? I have estimated it at thirty-five hundred dollars; but, frankly, I never get off with any such trifling sum. Our passage alone costs us from seven hundred to a thousand dollars, or even more and our ten-days' motor trip—the invariable climax of the expedition rendered necessary by the fatigue incident to shopping—at least five hundred dollars.

15

Our hotel bills in Paris, our taxicabs, theater tickets, and dinners at expensive restaurants cost us at least a thousand dollars, without estimating the total of those invariable purchases that are paid for out of the letter of credit and not charged to my wife's regular allowance. Even in Paris she will, without a thought, spend fifty dollars at Reboux' for a simple spring hat—and this is not regarded as expensive. Her dresses cost as much as if purchased on Fifth Avenue and I am obliged to pay a sixty per cent duty on them besides.

The restaurants of Paris—the chic ones—charge as much as those in New York; in fact, chic Paris exists very largely for the exploitation of the wives of rich Americans. The smart French woman buys no such dresses and pays no such prices. She knows a clever little modiste down some alley leading off the Rue St. Honoré who will saunter into Worth's, sweep the group of models with her eye, and go back to her own shop and turn out the latest fashions at a quarter of the money.

A French woman in society will have the same dress made for her by her own dressmaker for seventy dollars for which an American will cheerfully pay three hundred and fifty. And the reason is, that she has been taught from girlhood the relative values of things. She knows that mere clothes can never really take the place of charm and breeding; that expensive entertainments, no matter how costly and choice the viands, can never give equal pleasure with a cup of tea served with vivacity and wit; and that the best things of Paris are, in fact, free to all alike—the sunshine of the boulevards, the ever-changing spectacle of the crowds, the glamour of the evening glow beyond the Hôtel des Invalides, and the lure of the lamp-strewn twilight of the Champs Elysées.

So she gets a new dress or two and, after the three months of her season in the Capital are over, is content to lead a more or less simple family life in the country for the rest of the year. One rarely sees a real Parisian at one of the highly advertised all-night resorts of Paris. No Frenchman would pay the price.

An acquaintance of mine took his wife and a couple of friends one evening to what is known as L'Abbaye, in Montmartre. Knowing that it had a reputation for being expensive, he resisted, somewhat self-consciously, the delicate suggestions of the head waiter and ordered only one bottle of champagne, caviar for four, and a couple of cigars. After watching the dancing for an hour he called for his bill and found that the amount was two hundred and fifty francs. Rather than be conspicuous he paid it—foolishly. But the American who takes his wife abroad must have at least one vicarious taste of fast life, no matter what it costs, and he is a lucky fellow who can

16

save anything out of a bill of exchange that has cost him five thousand dollars.

After dispassionate consideration of the matter I hazard the sincere opinion that my actual disbursements during the last ten years have averaged not less than one hundred thousand dollars a year. However, let us be conservative and stick to our original figure of seventy-five thousand dollars. It costs me, therefore, almost exactly two hundred dollars a day to support five persons. We all of us complain of what is called the high cost of living, but men of my class have no real knowledge of what it costs them to live.

The necessaries are only a drop in the bucket. It is hardly worth while to bother over the price of rib roast a pound, or fresh eggs a dozen, when one is smoking fifty-cent cigars. Essentially it costs me as much to lunch off a boiled egg, served in my dining room at home, as to carve the breast off a canvasback. At the end of the month my bills would not show the difference. It is the overhead—or, rather, in housekeeping, the underground—charge that counts. That boiled egg or the canvasback represents a running expense of at least a hundred dollars a day. Slight variations in the cost of foodstuffs or servants' wages amount to practically nothing.

And what do I get for my two hundred dollars a day and my seventy-five thousand dollars a year that the other fellow does not enjoy for, let us say, half the money? Let us readjust the budget with an idea to ascertaining on what a family of five could live in luxury in the city of New York a year. I could rent a good house for five thousand dollars and one in the country for two thousand dollars; and I would have no real-estate taxes. I could keep eight trained servants for three thousand dollars and reduce the cost of my supplies to five thousand almost without knowing it. Of course my light and heat would cost me twelve hundred dollars and my automobile twenty-five hundred. My wife, daughters and son ought to be able to manage to dress on five thousand dollars, among them. I could give away fifteen hundred dollars and allow one thousand for doctors' bills, fifteen hundred for my own expenses, and still have twenty-three hundred for pleasure—and be living on thirty thousand dollars a year in luxury.

I could even then entertain, go to the theater, and occasionally take my friends to a restaurant. And what would I surrender? My saddle-horses, my extra motor, my pretentious houses, my opera box, my wife's annual spending bout in Paris—that is about all. And I would have a cash balance of forty-five thousand dollars.

REVISED BUDGET

Rent—City and country $7,000
Servants 3,000
Supplies 5,000
Light and heat 1,200
Motor 2,500
Allowance to family 5,000
Charity 1,500
Medical attendance 1,000
Self 1,500
Travel, pleasure, music and sundries 2,300

Total $30,000

In a smaller city I could do the same thing for half the money—fifteen thousand dollars; in Rome, Florence or Munich I could live like a prince on half the sum. I am paying apparently forty-five thousand dollars each year for the veriest frills of existence—for geranium powder in my bath, for fifteen extra feet in the width of my drawing room, for a seat in the parterre instead of the parquet at the opera, for the privilege of having a second motor roll up to the door when it is needed, and that my wife may have seven new evening dresses each winter instead of two. And in reality these luxuries mean nothing to me. I do not want them. I am not a whit more comfortable with than without them.

If an income tax should suddenly cut my bank account in half it would not seriously inconvenience me. No financial cataclasm, however dire, could deprive me of the genuine luxuries of my existence. Yet in my revised schedule of expenditure I would still be paying nearly a hundred dollars a day for the privilege of living. What would I be getting for my money—even then? What would I receive as a quid pro quo for my thirty thousand dollars?

I am not enough of a materialist to argue that my advantage over my less successful fellow man lies in having a bigger house, men servants instead of maid servants, and smoking cigars alleged to be from Havana instead of from Tampa; but I believe I am right in asserting that my social opportunities—in the broader sense—are vastly greater than his. I am meeting bigger men and have my fingers in bigger things. I give orders and he takes them.

My opinion has considerable weight in important matters,

some of which vitally affect large communities. My astuteness has put millions into totally unexpected pockets and defeated the faultily expressed intentions of many a testator. I can go to the White House and get an immediate hearing, and I can do more than that with judges of the Supreme Court in their private chambers.

In other words I am an active man of affairs, a man among men, a man of force and influence, who, as we say, "cuts ice" in the metropolis. But the economic weakness in the situation lies in the fact that a boiled egg only costs the ordinary citizen ten cents and it costs me almost its weight in gold.

Compare this de-luxe existence of mine with that of my forebears. We are assured by most biographers that the subject of their eulogies was born of poor but honest parents. My own parents were honest, but my father was in comfortable circumstances and was able to give me the advantages incident to an education, first at the local high school and later at college. I did not as a boy get up while it was still dark and break the ice in the horsetrough in order to perform my ablutions. I was, to be sure, given to understand—and always when a child religiously believed—that this was my father's unhappy fate. It may have been so, but I have a lingering doubt on the subject that refuses to be dissipated. I can hardly credit the idea that the son of the village clergyman was obliged to go through any such rigorous physical discipline as a child.

Even in 1820 there were such things as hired men and tradition declares that the one in my grandparents' employ was known as Jonas, had but one good eye and was half-witted. It modestly refrains from asserting that he had only one arm and one leg. My grandmother did the cooking—her children the housework; but Jonas was their only servant, if servant he can be called. It is said that he could perform wonders with an ax and could whistle the very birds off the trees.

Some time ago I came upon a trunkful of letters written by my grandfather to my father in 1835, when the latter was in college. They were closely written with a fine pen in a small, delicate hand, and the lines of ink, though faded, were like steel engraving. They were stilted, godly—in an ingenuous fashion—at times ponderously humorous, full of a mild self-satisfaction, and inscribed under the obvious impression that only the writer could save my father's soul from hell or his kidneys from destruction. The goodness of the Almighty, as exemplified by His personal attention to my grandfather, the efficacy of oil distilled from the liver of the cod, and the wisdom of Solomon, came in for an equal share of attention. How the good old gentleman must have enjoyed writing those letters! And, though I have never written my own son three letters

19

in my life, I suppose the desire of self-expression is stirring in me now these seventy-eight years later. I wonder what he would have said could he read these confessions of mine—he who married my grandmother on a capital of twenty-five dollars and enough bleached cotton to make half a dozen shirts! My annual income would have bought the entire county in which he lived. My son scraped through Harvard on twenty-five hundred dollars a year. I have no doubt that he left undisclosed liabilities behind him. Most of this allowance was spent on clothes, private commons and amusement. Lying before me is my father's term bill at college for the first half year of 1835. The items are:

To tuition $12.00
Room rent 3.00
Use of University Library 1.00
Servants' hire, printing, and so on 2.00
Repairs .80
Damage for glass .09
Commons bill, 15-1/2 weeks at $1.62 a week 25.11
Steward's salary 2.00
Public fuel .50
Absent from recitation without excuse—once .03

Total $46.53

The glass damage at nine cents and the three cents for absence without excuse give me joy. Father was human, after all!

Economically speaking, I do not think that his clothes cost him anything. He wore my grandfather's old ones. There were no amusements in those days, except going to see the pickled curios in the old Boston Museum. I have no doubt he drove to college in the family chaise—if there was one. I do not think that, in fact, there was.

On a conservative estimate he could not have cost my grandfather much, if anything, over a hundred dollars a year. On this basis I could, on my present income, send seven hundred and fifty fathers to college annually! A curious thought, is it not?

Undoubtedly my grandfather went barefoot and trudged many a weary mile, winter and summer, to and from the district school. He worked his way through college. He married and reared a family. He educated my father. He watched over his flock in

20

sickness and in health, and he died at a ripe old age, mourned by the entire countryside.

My father, in his turn, was obliged to carve out his own fate. He left the old home, moved to the town where I was born, and by untiring industry built up a law practice which for those days was astonishingly lucrative. Then, as I have said, the war broke out and, enlisting as a matter of course, he met death on the battlefield. During his comparatively short life he followed the frugal habits acquired in his youth. He was a simple man.

Yet I am his son! What would he say could he see my valet, my butler, my French cook? Would he admire and appreciate my paintings, my objets d'art, my rugs and tapestries, my rare old furniture? As an intelligent man he would undoubtedly have the good taste to realize their value and take satisfaction in their beauty; but would he be glad that I possessed them? That is a question. Until I began to pen these confessions I should have unhesitatingly answered it in the affirmative. Now I am inclined to wonder a little. I think it would depend on how far he believed that my treasures indicated on my own part a genuine love of art, and how far they were but the evidences of pomp and vainglory.

Let me be honest in the matter. I own some masterpieces of great value. At the time of their purchase I thought I had a keen admiration for them. I begin to suspect that I acquired them less because I really cared for such things than because I wished to be considered a connoisseur. There they hang—my Corots, my Romneys, my Teniers, my Daubignys. But they might as well be the merest chromos. I never look at them. I have forgotten that they exist. So have the rest of my family.

It is the same way with my porcelains and tapestries. Of course they go to make up the tout ensemble of a harmonious and luxurious home, but individually they mean nothing to me. I should not miss them if they were all swept out of existence tomorrow by a fire. I am no happier in my own house than in a hotel. My pictures are nothing but so much furniture requiring heavy insurance.

It is somewhat the same with our cuisine. My food supply costs me forty dollars a day. We use the choicest teas, the costliest caviar and relishes, the richest sterilized milk and cream, the freshest eggs, the choicest cuts of meat. We have course after course at lunch and dinner; yet I go to the table without an appetite and my food gives me little pleasure. But this style of living is the concrete expression of my success. Because I have risen above my fellows I must be surrounded by these tangible evidences of prosperity.

I get up about nine o'clock in the morning unless I have been out very late the night before, in which case I rest until ten or later. I step into a porcelain tub in which my servant has drawn a warm bath of water filtered by an expensive process which makes it as clear and blue as crystal. When I leave my bath my valet hands me one by one the garments that have been carefully laid out in order. He is always hovering round me, and I rather pride myself on the fact that I lace my own shoes and brush my own hair. Then he gives me a silk handkerchief and I stroll into my upstairs sitting room ready for breakfast.

My daughters are still sleeping. They rarely get up before eleven in the morning, and my wife and I do not, as a rule, breakfast together. We have tried that arrangement and found it wanting, for we are slightly irritable at this hour. My son has already gone downtown. So I enter the chintz-furnished room alone and sit down by myself before a bright wood fire and glance at the paper, which the valet has ironed, while I nibble an egg, drink a glass of orange juice, swallow a few pieces of toast and quaff a great cup of fragrant coffee.

Coffee! Goddess of the nerve-exhausted! Sweet invigorator of tired manhood! Savior of the American race! I could not live without you! One draft at your Pyrenean fountain and I am young again! For a moment the sun shines as it used to do in my boyhood's days; my blood quickens; I am eager to be off to business—to do, no matter what.

I enter the elevator and sink to the ground floor. My valet and butler are waiting, the former with my coat over his arm, ready to help me into it. Then he hands me my hat and stick, while the butler opens the front door and escorts me to my motor. The chauffeur touches his hat. I light a small and excellent Havana cigar and sink back among the cushions. The interior of the car smells faintly of rich upholstery and violet perfume. My daughters have been to a ball the night before. If it is fine I have the landaulette hood thrown open and take the air as far as Washington Square—if not, I am deposited at the Subway.

Ten o'clock sees me at my office. The effect of the coffee has begun to wear off slightly. I am a little peevish with my secretary, who has opened and arranged all my letters on my desk. There are a pile of dividend checks, a dozen appeals for charity and a score of letters relating to my business. I throw the begging circulars into the waste-basket and dictate most of my answers in a little over half an hour. Then come a stream of appointments until lunchtime.

On the top floor of a twenty-story building, its windows commanding a view of all the waters surrounding the end of Manhattan Island, is my lunch club. Here gather daily at one o'clock most of the men with whom I am associated—bankers, railroad promoters and other lawyers. I lunch with one or more of them. A cocktail starts my appetite, for I have no desire for food; and for the sake of appearances I manage to consume an egg Benedictine and a ragout of lamb, with a dessert.

Then we wander into the smoking room and drink black coffee and smoke long black cigars. I have smoked a cigar or two in my office already and am beginning, as usual, to feel a trifle seedy. Here we plan some piece of business or devise a method of escaping the necessity of fulfilling some corporate obligation.

Two or half-past finds me in my office again. The back of the day is broken. I take things more easily. Later on I smoke another cigar. I discuss general matters with my junior partners. At half-past four I enter my motor, which is waiting at the Wall Street entrance of the building. At my uptown club the men are already dropping in and gathering round the big windows. We all call each other by our first names, yet few of us know anything of one another's real character. We have a bluff heartiness, a cheerful cynicism that serves in place of sincerity, and we ask no questions.

Our subjects of conversation are politics, the stock market, "big" business, and the more fashionable sports. There is no talk of art or books, no discussion of subjects of civic interest. After our cocktails we usually arrange a game of bridge and play until it is time to go home to dress for dinner.

Until this time, usually, I have not met my wife and daughters since the night before. They have had their own individual engagements for luncheon and in the afternoon, and perhaps have not seen each other before during the day. But we generally meet at least two or three times a week on the stairs or in the hall as we are going out. Sometimes, also, I see my son at this time.

It will be observed that our family life is not burdensome to any of us:—not that we do not wish to see one another, but we are too busy to do so. My daughters seem to be fond of me. They are proud of my success and their own position; in fact they go out in the smartest circles. They are smarter, indeed, than their mother and myself; for, though we know everybody in society, we have never formed a part of the intimate inner Newport circle. But my daughters are inside and in the very center of the ring. You can read their names as present at every smart function that takes place.

From Friday until Monday they are always in the country at week-end parties. They are invited to go to Bermuda, Palm Beach, California, Aiken and the Glacier National Park. They live on yachts and in private cars and automobiles. They know all the patter of society and everything about everybody. They also talk surprisingly well about art, music and international politics. They are as much at home in Rome, Paris and London as they are in New York, and are as familiar with Scotland as Long Island. They constantly amaze me by the apparent scope of their information.

They are women of the world in a sense unheard of by my father's generation. They have been presented at court in London, Berlin and Rome, and have had a social season at Cairo; in fact I feel at a great personal disadvantage in talking with them. They are respectful, very sweet in a self-controlled and capable sort of way, and, so far as I can see, need no assistance in looking out for themselves. They seem to be quite satisfied with their mode of life. They do as they choose, and ask for no advice from either their mother or myself.

My boy also leads his own life. He is rarely at home except to sleep. I see less of him than of my daughters. During the day he is at the office, where he is learning to be a lawyer. At wide intervals we lunch together; but I find that he is interested in things which do not appeal to me at all. Just at present he has become an expert— almost a professional—dancer to syncopated music. I hear of him as dancing for charity at public entertainments, and he is in continual demand for private theatricals and parties. He is astonishingly clever at it.

Yet I cannot imagine Daniel Webster or Rufus Choate dancing in public even in their leisure moments. Perhaps, however, it is better for him to dance than to do some other things. It is good exercise; and, to be fair with him, I cannot imagine Choate or Webster playing bridge or taking scented baths. But, frankly, it is a far cry from my clergyman grandfather to my ragtime dancing offspring. Perhaps, however, the latter will serve his generation in his own way.

It may seem incredible that a father can be such a stranger to his children, but it is none the less a fact. I do not suppose we dine together as a family fifteen times in the course of the winter. When we do so we get along together very nicely, but I find myself conversing with my daughters much as if they were women I had met casually out at dinner. They are literally "perfect ladies."

When they were little I was permitted a certain amount of decorous informality, but now I have to be very careful how I kiss them on account of the amount of powder they use. They have, both of them, excellent natural complexions, but they are not satisfied unless their noses have an artificial whiteness like that of marble. I suspect, also, that their lips have a heightened color. At all events I am careful to "mind the paint." But they are—either because of these things or in spite of them—extraordinarily pretty girls— prettier, I am forced to admit, than their mother was at their age.

Now, as I write, I wonder to what end these children of mine have been born into the world—how they will assist in the development of the race to a higher level.

For years I slaved at the office—early, late, in the evenings, often working Sundays and holidays, and foregoing my vacation in the summer.

Then came the period of expansion. My accumulations doubled and trebled. In one year I earned a fee in a railroad reorganization of two hundred thousand dollars. I found myself on Easy Street. I had arrived—achieved my success. During all those years I had devoted myself exclusively to the making of money. Now I simply had to spend it and go through the motions of continuing to work at my profession.

My wife and I became socially ambitious. She gave herself to this end eventually with the same assiduity I had displayed at the law. It is surprising at the present time to recall that it was not always easy to explain the ultimate purpose in view. Alas! What is it now? Is it other than that expressed by my wife on the occasion when our youngest daughter rebelled at having to go to a children's party?

"Why must I go to parties?" she insisted.

"In order," replied her mother, "that you may be invited to other parties."

It was the unconscious epitome of my consort's theory of the whole duty of man.

25

CHAPTER II

MY FRIENDS

By virtue of my being a successful man my family has an established position in New York society. We are not, to be sure—at least, my wife and I are not—a part of the sacrosanct fifty or sixty who run the show and perform in the big ring; but we are well up in the front of the procession and occasionally do a turn or so in one of the side rings. We give a couple of dinners each week during the season and a ball or two, besides a continuous succession of opera and theater parties.

Our less desirable acquaintances, and those toward whom we have minor social obligations, my wife disposes of by means of an elaborate "at home," where the inadequacies of the orchestra are drowned in the roar of conversation, and which a sufficient number of well-known people are good-natured enough to attend in order to make the others feel that the occasion is really smart and that they are not being trifled with. This method of getting rid of one's shabby friends and their claims is, I am informed, known as "killing them off with a tea."

We have a slaughter of this kind about once in two years. In return for these courtesies we are invited yearly by the élite to some two hundred dinners, about fifty balls and dances, and a large number of miscellaneous entertainments such as musicales, private theatricals, costume affairs, bridge, poker, and gambling parties; as well as in the summer to clambakes—where champagne and terrapin are served by footmen—and other elegant rusticities.

Besides these chic functions we are, of course, deluged with invitations to informal meals with old and new friends, studio parties, afternoon teas, highbrow receptions and conversaziones, reformers' lunch parties, and similar festivities. We have cut out all these long ago. Keeping up with our smart acquaintances takes all our energy and available time. There are several old friends of mine on the next block to ours whom I have not met socially for nearly ten years.

We have definitely arrived however. There is no question about that. We are in society and entitled to all the privileges pertaining thereto. What are they? you ask. Why, the privilege of going to all these balls, concerts and dinners, of course; of calling the men and women one reads about in the paper by their first names; of having the satisfaction of knowing that everybody who knows anything knows we are in society; and of giving our daughters and son the chance to enjoy, without any effort on their part, these same privileges that their parents have spent a life of effort to secure.

Incidentally, I may add, our offspring will, each of them—if I am not very much mistaken—marry money, since I have observed a certain frankness on their part in this regard, which seems to point that way and which, if not admirable in itself, at least does credit to their honesty.

Now it is undubitably the truth that my wife regards our place among the socially elect as the crowning achievement—the great desideratum—of our joint career. It is what we have always been striving for. Without it we—both of us—would have unquestionably acknowledged failure. My future, my reputation, my place at the bar and my domestic life would have meant nothing at all to us, had not the grand cordon of success been thrown across our shoulders by society.

* * * * *

As I have achieved my ambition in this respect it is no small part of my self-imposed task to somewhat analyze this, the chief reward of my devotion to my profession, my years of industrious application, my careful following of the paths that other successful Americans have blazed for me.

I must confess at the outset that it is ofttimes difficult to determine where the pleasure ends and work begins. Even putting it in this way, I fear I am guilty of a euphemism; for, now that I consider the matter honestly, I recall no real pleasure or satisfaction derived from the various entertainments I have attended during the last five or ten years.

In the first place I am invariably tired when I come home at night—less perhaps from the actual work I have done at my office than from the amount of tobacco I have consumed and the nervous strain attendant on hurrying from one engagement to another and keeping up the affectation of hearty good-nature which is part of my stock in trade. At any rate, even if my body is not tired, my head, nerves and eyes are distinctly so.

I often feel, when my valet tells me that the motor is ordered at ten minutes to eight, that I would greatly enjoy having him slip into the dress-clothes he has so carefully laid out on my bed and go out to dinner in my place. He would doubtless make himself quite

27

as agreeable as I. And then—let me see—what would I do? I sit with one of my accordion-plaited silk socks half on and surrender myself to all the delights of the most reckless imagination!

Yes, what would I choose if I could do anything in the world for the next three hours? First, I think, I would like an egg—a poached egg, done just right, like a little snowball, balanced nicely in the exact center of a hot piece of toast! My mouth waters. Aunt Jane used to do them like that. And then I would like a crisp piece of gingerbread and a glass of milk. Dress? Not on your life! Where is that old smoking-jacket of mine? Not the one with Japanese embroidery on it—no; the old one. Given away? I groan aloud.

Well, the silk one will have to do—and a pair of comfortable slippers! Where is that old brier pipe I keep to go a-fishing? Now I want a book—full of the sea and ships—of pirates and coral reefs—yes, Treasure Island; of course that's it—and Long John Silver and the Black Spot.

"Beg pardon, sir, but madam has sent me up to say the motor is waiting," admonishes my English footman respectfully.

Gone—gone is my poached egg, my pipe, my dream of the Southern Seas! I dash into my evening clothes under the solicitous guidance of my valet and hastily descend in the electric elevator to the front hall. My wife has already taken her seat in the motor, with an air of righteous annoyance, of courteously suppressed irritation. The butler is standing on the doorstep. The valet is holding up my fur coat expectantly. I am sensible of an atmosphere of sad reproachfulness.

Oh, well! I thrust my arms into my coat, grasp my white gloves and cane, receive my hat and wearily start forth on my evening's task of being entertained; conscious as I climb into the motor that this curious form of so-called amusement has certain rather obvious limitations.

For what is its raison d'être? It is obvious that if I know any persons whose society and conversation are likely to give me pleasure I can invite them to my own home and be sure of an evening's quiet enjoyment. But, so far as I can see, my wife does not invite to our house the people who are likely to give either her or myself any pleasure at all, and neither am I likely to meet such people at the homes of my friends.

The whole thing is a mystery governed by strange laws and curious considerations of which I am kept in utter ignorance; in fact, I rarely know where I am going to dine until I arrive at the house. On several occasions I have come away without having any very clear idea as to where I have been.

"The Hobby-Smiths," my wife will whisper as we go up the

steps. "Of course you've heard of her! She is a great friend of Marie Van Duser, and her husband is something in Wall Street."

That is a comparatively illuminating description. At all events it insures some remote social connection with ourselves, if only through Miss Van Duser and Wall Street. Most of our hosts are something in Wall Street. Occasionally they are something in coal, iron, oil or politics.

I find a small envelope bearing my name on a silver tray by the hatstand and open it suspiciously as my wife is divested of her wraps. Inside is a card bearing in an almost illegible scrawl the words: Mrs. Jones. I hastily refresh my recollection as to all the Joneses of my acquaintance, whether in coal, oil or otherwise; but no likely candidate for the distinction of being the husband of my future dinner companion comes to my mind. Yet there is undoubtedly a Jones. But, no! The lady may be a divorcée or a widow. I recall no Mrs. Jones, but I visualize various possible Miss Joneses—ladies very fat and bursting; ladies scrawny, lean and sardonic; facetious ladies; heavy, intelligent ladies; aggressive, militant ladies.

My spouse has turned away from the mirror and the butler has pulled back the portières leading into the drawing room. I follow my wife's composed figure as she sweeps toward our much-beplumed hostess and find myself in a roomful of heterogeneous people, most of whom I have never seen before and whose personal appearance is anything but encouraging.

"This is very nice!" says our hostess—accent on the nice.

"So nice of you to think of us!" answers my wife.

We shake hands and smile vaguely. The butler rattles the portières and two more people come in.

"This is very nice!" says the hostess again—accent on the is.

It may be here noted that at the conclusion of the evening each guest murmurs in a simpering, half-persuasive yet consciously deprecatory manner—as if apologizing for the necessity of so bald a prevarication—"Good-night! We have had such a good time! So good of you to ask us!" This epilogue never changes. Its phrase is cast and set. The words may vary slightly, but the tone, emphasis and substance are inviolable. Yet, disregarding the invocation good-night! the fact remains that neither have you had a good time nor was your host in any way good or kind in asking you.

Returning to the moment at which you have made your entrance and been received and passed along, you gaze vaguely round you at the other guests, greeting those you know with exaggerated enthusiasm and being the conscious subject of whispered criticism and inquiry on the part of the others. You make

29

your way to the side of a lady whom you have previously encountered at a similar entertainment and assert your delight at revamping the fatuous acquaintanceship. Her facetiousness is elephantine, but the relief of conversation is such that you laugh loudly at her witticisms and simper knowingly at her platitudes—both of which have now been current for several months.

The edge of your delight is, however, somewhat dulled by the discovery that she is the lady whom fate has ordained that you shall take in to dinner—a matter of which you were sublimely unconscious owing to the fact that you had entirely forgotten her name. As the couples pair off to march to the dining room and the combinations of which you may form a possible part are reduced to a scattering two or three, you realize with a shudder that the lady beside you is none other than Mrs. Jones—and that for the last ten minutes you have been recklessly using up the evening's conversational ammunition.

With a sinking heart you proffer your arm, wondering whether it will be possible to get through the meal and preserve the fiction of interest. You wish savagely that you could turn on her and exclaim honestly:

"Look here, my good woman, you are all right enough in your own way, but we have nothing in common; and this proposed evening of enforced companionship will leave us both exhausted and ill-tempered. We shall grin and shout meaningless phrases over the fish, entrée and salad about life, death and the eternal verities; but we shall be sick to death of each other in ten minutes. Let's cut it out and go home!"

You are obliged, however, to escort your middle-aged comrade downstairs and take your seat beside her with a flourish, as if you were playing Rudolph to her Flavia. Then for two hours, with your eyes blinded by candlelight and electricity, you eat recklessly as you grimace first over your left shoulder and then over your right. It is a foregone conclusion that you will have a headache by the time you have turned, with a sensation of momentary relief, to your "fair companion" on the other side.

Have you enjoyed yourself? Have you been entertained? Have you profited? The questions are utterly absurd. You have suffered. You have strained your eyes, overloaded your stomach, and wasted three hours during which you might have been recuperating from your day's work or really amusing yourself with people you like.

This entirely conventional form of amusement is, I am told, quite unknown in Europe. There are, to be sure, occasional formal banquets, which do not pretend to be anything but formal. A formal banquet would be an intense relief, after the heat, noise, confusion and pseudo-informality of a New York dinner. The European is puzzled and baffled by one of our combined talk-and-eating bouts.

A nobleman from Florence recently said to me:

"At home, when we go to other people's houses it is for the purpose of meeting our own friends or our friend's friends. We go after our evening meal and stay as long as we choose. Some light refreshment is served, and those who wish to do so smoke or play cards. The old and the young mingle together. It is proper for each guest to make himself agreeable to all the others. We do not desire to spend money or to make a fête. At the proper times we have our balls and festas.

"But here in New York each night I have been pressed to go to a grand entertainment and eat a huge dinner cooked by a French chef and served by several men servants, where I am given one lady to talk to for several hours. I must converse with no one else, even if there is a witty, beautiful and charming woman directly opposite me; and as I talk and listen I must consume some ten or twelve courses or fail to do justice to my host's hospitality. I am given four or five costly wines, caviar, turtle soup, fish, mousse, a roast, partridge, pâté de fois gras, glacés, fruits, bonbons, and cigars costing two francs each. Not to eat and drink would be to insult the friend who is paying at least forty or fifty francs for my dinner. But I cannot enjoy a meal eaten in such haste and I cannot enjoy talking to one strange lady for so long.

"Then the men retire to a chamber from which the ladies are excluded. I must talk to some man. Perhaps I have seen an attractive woman I wish to meet. It is hopeless. I must talk to her husband! At the end of three-quarters of an hour the men march to the drawing room, and again I talk to some one lady for half an hour and then must go home! It may be only half-past ten o'clock, but I have no choice. Away I must go. I say good-night. I have eaten a huge dinner; I have talked to one man and three ladies; I have drunk a great deal of wine and my head is very tired.

"Nineteen other people have had the same experience, and it has cost my host from five hundred to a thousand francs—or, as you say here, from one hundred to two hundred dollars. And why has he spent this sum of money? Pardon me, my friend, if I say that it could be disbursed to much better advantage. Should my host come to Florence I should not dare to ask him to dinner, for we cannot afford to have these elaborate functions. If he came to my house he would have to dine en famille. Here you feast every night in the winter. Why? Every day is not a feast day!"

I devote space and time to this subject commensurate with what seems to me to be its importance. Dining out is the

31

metropolitan form of social entertainment for the well-to-do. I go to such affairs at least one hundred nights each year. That is a large proportion of my whole life and at least one-half of all the time at my disposal for recreation. So far as I can see, it is totally useless and a severe drain on one's nervous centers. It has sapped and is sapping my vitality. During the winter I am constantly tired. My head aches a large part of the time. I can do only a half—and on some days only a third—as much work as I could at thirty-five.

I wake with a thin, fine line of pain over my right eye, and a heavy head. A strong cup of coffee sets me up and I feel better; but as the morning wears on, especially if I am nervous, the weariness in my head returns. By luncheon time I am cross and upset. Often by six o'clock I have a severe sick headache. When I do not have a headache I am usually depressed; my brain feels like a lump of lead. And I know precisely the cause: It is that I do not give my nerve-centers sufficient rest. If I could spend the evenings—or half of them—quietly I should be well enough; but after I am tired out by a day's work I come home only to array myself to go out to saw social wood.

I never get rested! My head gets heavier and heavier and finally gives way. There is no immediate cause. It is the fact that my nervous system gets more and more tired without any adequate relief. The feeling of complete restedness, so far as my brain is concerned, is one I almost never experience. When I do wake up with my head clear and light my heart sings for joy. My effectiveness is impaired by weariness and overeating, through a false effort at recuperation. I have known this for a long time, but I have seen no escape from it.

Social life is one of the objects of living in New York; and social life to ninety per cent of society people means nothing but eating one another's dinners. Men never pay calls or go to teas. The dinner, which has come to mean a heavy, elaborate meal, eaten amid noise, laughter and chatter, at great expense, is the expression of our highest social aspirations. Thus it would seem, though I had not thought of it before, that I work seven or eight hours every day in order to make myself rather miserable for the rest of the time.

"I am going to lie down and rest this afternoon," my wife will sometimes say. "We're dining with the Robinsons."

Extraordinary that pleasure should be so exhausting as to require rest in anticipation! Dining with these particular and other in-general Robinsons has actually become a physical feat of endurance—a tour de force, like climbing the Matterhorn or eating thirteen pounds of beefsteak at a sitting. Is it a reminiscence of those dim centuries when our ancestors in the forests of the Elbe sat

32

under the moss-hung oaks and stuffed themselves with roast ox washed down with huge skins of wine? Or is it a custom born of those later days when, round the blazing logs of Canadian campfires, our Indian allies gorged themselves into insensibility to the sound of the tom-tom and the chant of the medicine-man—the latter quite as indispensable now as then?

If I should be called on to explain for what reason I am accustomed to eat not wisely but too well on these joyous occasions, I should be somewhat at a loss for any adequate reply. Perhaps the simplest answer would be that I have just imbibed a cocktail and created an artificial appetite. It is also probable that, in my efforts to appear happy and at ease, to play my part as a connoisseur of good things, and to keep the conversational ball in the air, I unconsciously lose track of the number of courses I have consumed.

It is also a matter of habit. As a boy I was compelled to eat everything on my plate; and as I grew older I discovered that in our home town it was good manners to leave nothing undevoured and thus pay a concrete tribute to the culinary ability of the hostess. Be that as it may, I have always liked to eat. It is almost the only thing left that I enjoy; but, even so, my palate requires the stimulus of gin. I know that I am getting fat. My waistcoats have to be let out a little more every five or six months. Anyhow, if the men did not do their part there would be little object for giving dinner parties in these days when slender women are the fashion.

After the long straight front and the habit back, social usage is frowning on the stomach, hips and other heretofore not unadmired evidences of robust nutrition. Temperance, not to say total abstinence, has become de rigueur among the ladies. My dinner companion nibbles her celery, tastes the soup, waves away fish, entrée and roast, pecks once or twice at the salad, and at last consumes her ration of ice-cream with obvious satisfaction. If there is a duck—well, she makes an exception in the case of duck—at six dollars and a half a pair. A couple of hothouse grapes and she is done.

It will be observed that this gives her all the more opportunity for conversation—a doubtful blessing. On the other hand, there is an equivalent economic waste. I have no doubt each guest would prefer to have set before her a chop, a baked potato and a ten-dollar goldpiece. It would amount to the same thing, so far as the host is concerned.

＊ ＊ ＊ ＊ ＊

I had, until recently, assumed with some bitterness that my

33

dancing days were over. My wife and I went to balls, to be sure, but not to dance. We left that to the younger generation, for the reason that my wife did not care to jeopardize her attire or her complexion. She was also conscious of the fact that the variety of waltz popular thirty years ago was an oddity, and that a middle-aged woman who went hopping and twirling about a ballroom must be callous to the amusement that followed her gyrations.

With the advent of the turkey trot and the tango, things have changed however. No one is too stout, too old or too clumsy to go walking solemnly round, in or out of time to the music. I confess to a consciousness of absurdity when, to the exciting rhythm of Très Moutard, I back Mrs. Jones slowly down the room and up again.

"Do you grapevine?" she inquires ardently. Yes; I admit the soft impeachment, and at once she begins some astonishing convolutions with the lower part of her body, which I attempt to follow. After several entanglements we move triumphantly across the hall.

"How beautifully you dance!" she pants.

Aged roisterer that I am, I fall for the compliment. She is a nice old thing, after all!

"Fish walk?" asks she.

I retort with total abandon.

"Come along!"

So, grabbing her tightly and keeping my legs entirely stiff—as per instructions from my son—I stalk swiftly along the floor, while she backs with prodigious velocity. Away we go, an odd four hundred pounds of us, until, exhausted, we collapse against the table where the champagne is being distributed.

Though I have carefully followed the directions of my preceptor, I am aware that the effect produced by our efforts is somehow not the same as his. I observe him in a close embrace with a willowy young thing, dipping gracefully in the distance. They pause, sway, run a few steps, stop dead and suddenly sink to the floor—only to rise and repeat the performance.

So the evening wears gaily on. I caper round—now sedately, now deliriously—knowing that, however big a fool I am making of myself, we are all in the same boat. My wife is doing it, too, to the obvious annoyance of our daughters. But this is the smartest ball of the season. When all the world is dancing it would be conspicuous to loiter in the doorway. Society has ruled that I must dance—if what I am doing can be so called.

I am aware that I should not care to allow my clients to catch an unexpected glimpse of my antics with Mrs. Jones; yet to be permitted to dance with her is one of the privileges of our success. I might dance elsewhere but it would not be the same thing. Is not my hostess' hoarse, good-natured, rather vulgar voice the clarion of society? Did not my wife scheme and plot for years before she managed to get our names on the sacred list of invitations?

To be sure, I used to go to dances enough as a lad; and good times I had too. The High School Auditorium had a splendid floor; and the girls, even though they were unacquainted with all these newfangled steps, could waltz and polka, and do Sir Roger de Coverley. Good old days! I remember my wife—met her in that old hall. She wore a white muslin dress trimmed with artificial roses. I wonder if I properly appreciate the distinction of being asked to Mrs. Jones' turkey-trotting parties! My butler and the kitchen-maid are probably doing the same thing in the basement at home to the notes of the usefulman's accordion—and having a better time than I am.

It is a pleasure to watch my son or my daughters glide through the intricacies of these modern dances, which the natural elasticity and suppleness of youth render charming in spite of their grotesqueness. But why should I seek to copy them? In spite of the fact that I am still rather athletic I cannot do so. With my utmost endeavor I fail to imitate their grace. I am getting old. My muscles are stiff and out of training. My wind has suffered. Mrs. Jones probably never had any.

And if I am ridiculous, what of her and the other women of her age who, for some unknown reason, fatuously suppose they can renew their lost youth? Occasionally luck gives me a débutante for a partner when I go out to dinner. I do my best to entertain her—trot out all my old jokes and stories, pay her delicate compliments, and do frank homage to her youth and beauty. But her attention wanders. My tongue is stiff, like my legs. It can wag through the old motions, but it has lost its spontaneity. One glance from the eye of the boy down the long table and she is oblivious of my existence. Should I try to dance with her I should quickly find that crabbed middle-age and youth cannot step in time. My place is with Mrs. Jones—or, better, at home and in bed.

Apart, however, from the dubious delight of dancing, all is not gold that glitters socially. The first time my wife and I were invited to a week-end party at the country-house of a widely known New York hostess we were both much excited. At last we were to be received on a footing of real intimacy by one of the inner circle. Even my valet, an imperturbable Englishman who would have announced that the house was on fire in the same tone as that my breakfast was ready, showed clearly that he was fully aware of the significance of the coming event. For several days he exhibited signs

35

of intense nervous anxiety, and when at last the time of my departure arrived I found that he had filled two steamer trunks with the things he regarded as indispensable for my comfort and well-being.

My wife's maid had been equally assiduous. Both she and the valet had no intention of learning on our return that any feature of our respective wardrobes had been forgotten; since we had decided not to take either of our personal servants, for the reason that we thought to do so might possibly be regarded as an ostentation.

I made an early getaway from my office on Friday afternoon, met my wife at the ferry, and in due course, but by no means with comfort, managed to board the train and secure our seats in the parlor car before it started. We reached our destination at about half-past four and were met by a footman in livery, who piloted us to a limousine driven by a French chauffeur. We were the only arrivals.

In my confusion I forgot to do anything about our trunks, which contained our evening apparel. During the run to the house we were both on the verge of hysteria owing to the speed at which we were driven—seventy miles an hour at the least. And at one corner we were thrown forward, clear of the seats and against the partition, by an unexpected stop. An interchange of French profanity tinted the atmosphere for a few moments and then we resumed the trajectory of our flight.

We had expected to be welcomed by our hostess; but instead we were informed by the butler that she and the other guests had driven over to watch a polo game and would probably not be back before six. As we had nothing to do we strolled round the grounds and looked at the shrubbery for a couple of hours, at the end of which period we had tea alone in the library. We had, of course, no sooner finished than the belated party entered, the hostess full of vociferous apologies.

I remember this occasion vividly because it was my first introduction to that artificially enforced merriment which is the inevitable concomitant of smart gatherings in America. The men invariably addressed each other as Old Man and the women as My Dear. No one was mentioned except by his or her first name or by some intimate diminutive or abbreviation. It seemed to be assumed that the guests were only interested in personal gossip relating to the marital infelicities of the neighboring countryside, who lost most at cards, and the theater. Every remark relating to these absorbing subjects was given a feebly humorous twist and greeted with a burst of hilarity. Even the mere suggestion of going upstairs to dress for dinner was a sufficient reason for an explosion of merriment. If noise was an evidence of having a good time these people were having the time of their lives. Personally I felt a little out of my element. I had still a lingering disinclination to pretend to a ubiquity of social acquaintance that I did not really possess, and I had never learned to laugh in a properly boisterous manner. But my wife appeared highly gratified.

Delay in sending to the depot for our trunks—the fault of the butler, to whom we turned over our keys—prevented, as we supposed, our getting ready in time for dinner. Everybody else had gone up to dress; so we also went to our rooms, which consisted of two huge apartments connected by a bathroom of similar acreage. The furniture was dainty and chintz-covered. There was an abundance of writing paper, envelopes, magazines and French novels. Superficially the arrangements were wholly charming.

The baggage arrived at about ten minutes to eight, after we had sat helplessly waiting for nearly an hour. The rooms were plentifully supplied with buttons marked: Maid; Valet; Butler's Pantry—and so on. But, though we pressed these anxiously, there was no response. I concluded that the valet was hunting or sleeping or otherwise occupied. I unpacked my trunks without assistance; my wife unpacked hers. But before I could find and assemble my evening garments I had to unwrap the contents of every tray and fill the room knee-high with tissue-paper.

Unable to secure any response to her repeated calls for the maid, my wife was nearly reduced to tears. However, in those days I was not unskillful in hooking up a dress, and we managed to get downstairs, with ready apologies on our lips, by twenty minutes of nine. We were the first ones down however.

The party assembled in a happy-go-lucky manner and, after the cocktails had been served, gathered round the festive board at five minutes past nine. The dinner was the regulation heavy, expensive New York meal, eaten to the accompaniment of the same noisy mirth I have already described. Afterward the host conducted the men to his "den," a luxurious paneled library filled with rare prints, and we listened for an hour to the jokes and anecdotes of a semiprofessional jester who took it on himself to act as the life of the party. It was after eleven o'clock when we rejoined the ladies, but the evening apparently had only just begun; the serious business of the day—bridge—was at hand. But in those days my wife and I did not play bridge; and as there was nothing else for us to do we retired, after a polite interval, to our apartments.

While getting ready for the night we shouted cheerfully to one another through the open doors of the bathroom and, I remember, became quite jolly; but when my wife had gone to bed and I tried to

37

close the blinds I discovered that there were none. Now neither of us had acquired the art of sleeping after daylight unless the daylight was excluded. With grave apprehension I arranged a series of makeshift screens and extinguished the lights, wandering round the room and turning off the key of each one separately, since the architect had apparently forgotten to put in a central switch.

If there had been no servants in evidence when we wanted them before dinner, no such complaint could be entered now. There seemed to be a bowling party going on upstairs. We could also hear plainly the rattle of dishes and a lively interchange of informalities from the kitchen end of the establishment. We lay awake tensely. Shortly after one o'clock these particular sounds died away, but there was a steady tramp of feet over our heads until three. About this hour, also, the bridge party broke up and the guests came upstairs.

There were no outside doors to our rooms. Bells rang, water ran, and there was that curious vibration which even hairbrushing seems to set going in a country house. Then with a final bang, comparative silence descended. Occasionally still, to be sure, the floor squeaked over our heads. Once somebody got up and closed a window. I could hear two distant snorings in major and minor keys. I managed to snatch a few winks and then an alarm-clock went off. At no great distance the scrubbing maid was getting up. I could hear her every move.

The sun also rose and threw fire-pointed darts at us through the windowshades. By five o'clock I was ready to scream with nerves; and, having dug a lounge suit out of the gentlemen's furnishing store in my trunk, I cautiously descended into the lower regions. There was a rich smell of cigarettes everywhere. In the hall I stumbled over the feet of the sleeping night-watchman. But the birds were twittering in the bushes; the grassblades threw back a million flashes to the sun.

Not before a quarter to ten could I secure a cup of coffee, though several footmen, in answer to my insistent bell, had been running round apparently for hours in a vain endeavor to get it for me. At eleven a couple of languid younger men made their appearance and conversed apathetically with one another over the papers. The hours drew on.

Lunch came at two o'clock, bursting like a thunder-storm out of a sunlit sky. Afterward the guests sat round and talked. People were coming to tea at five, and there was hardly any use in doing anything before that time. A few took naps. A young lady and gentleman played an impersonal game of tennis; but at five an avalanche of social leaders poured out of a dozen shrieking motors and stormed the castle with salvos of strident laughter. The cannonade continued, with one brief truce in which to dress for dinner, until long after midnight. Vox, et praeterea nihil!

I look back on that house party with vivid horror. Yet it was one of the most valuable of my social experiences. We were guests invited for the first time to one of the smartest houses on Long Island; yet we were neglected by male and female servants alike, deprived of all possibility of sleep, and not the slightest effort was made to look after our personal comfort and enjoyment by either our host or hostess. Incidentally on my departure I distributed about forty dollars among various dignitaries who then made their appearance.

It is probable that time has somewhat exaggerated my recollections of the miseries of this our first adventure into ultrasmart society, but its salient characteristics have since repeated themselves in countless others. I no longer accept week-end invitations;—for me the quiet of my library or the Turkish bath at my club; for they are all essentially alike. Surrounded by luxury, the guests yet know no comfort!

After a couple of days of ennui and an equal number of sleepless nights, his brain foggy with innumerable drinks, his eyes dizzy with the pips of playing cards, and his ears still echoing with senseless hilarity, the guest rises while it is not yet dawn, and, fortified by a lukewarm cup of faint coffee boiled by the kitchen maid and a slice of leatherlike toast left over from Sunday's breakfast, presses ten dollars on the butler and five on the chauffeur—and boards the train for the city, nervous, disgruntled, his digestion upset and his head totally out of kilter for the day's work.

Since my first experience in house parties I have yielded weakly to my wife's importunities on several hundred similar occasions. Some of these visits have been fairly enjoyable. Sleep is sometimes possible. Servants are not always neglectful. Discretion in the matter of food and drink is conceivable, even if not probable, and occasionally one meets congenial persons.

As a rule, however, all the hypocrisies of society are intensified threefold when heterogeneous people are thrown into the enforced contact of a Sunday together in the country; but the artificiality and insincerity of smart society is far less offensive than the pretentiousness of mere wealth.

* * * * *

Not long ago I attended a dinner given on Fifth Avenue the

invitation to which had been eagerly awaited by my wife. We were asked to dine informally with a middle-aged couple who for no obvious reason have been accepted as fashionable desirables. He is the retired head of a great combination of capital usually described as a trust. A canopy and a carpet covered the sidewalk outside the house. Two flunkies in cockaded hats stood beside the door, and in the hall was a line of six liveried lackeys. Three maids helped my wife remove her wraps and adjust her hair.

In the salon where our hostess received us were hung pictures representing an outlay of nearly two million dollars—part of a collection the balance of which they keep in their house in Paris; for these people are not content with one mansion on Fifth Avenue and a country house on Long Island, but own a palace overlooking the Bois de Boulogne and an enormous estate in Scotland. They spend less than ten weeks in New York, six in the country, and the rest of the year abroad.

The other male guests had all amassed huge fortunes and had given up active work. They had been, in their time, in the thick of the fray. Yet these men, who had swayed the destinies of the industrial world, stood about awkwardly discussing the most trivial of banalities, as if they had never had a vital interest in anything.

Then the doors leading into the dining room were thrown open, disclosing a table covered with rosetrees in full bloom five feet in height and a concealed orchestra began to play. There were twenty-four seats and a footman for each two chairs, besides two butlers, who directed the service. The dinner consisted of hors-d'oeuvre and grapefruit, turtle soup, fish of all sorts, elaborate entrées, roasts, breasts of plover served separately with salad, and a riot of ices and exotic fruits.

Throughout the meal the host discoursed learnedly on the relative excellence of various vintages of champagne and the difficulty of procuring cigars suitable for a gentleman to smoke. It appeared that there was no longer any wine—except a few bottles in his own cellar—which was palatable or healthful. Even coffee was not fit for use unless it had been kept for six years! His own cigars were made to order from a selected crop of tobacco he had bought up entire. His cigarettes, which were the size of small sausages, were prepared from specially cured leaves of plants grown on "sunny corners of the walls of Smyrna." His Rembrandts, his Botticellis, his Sir Joshuas, his Hoppners, were little things he had picked up here and there, but which, he admitted, were said to be rather good.

Soon all the others were talking wine, tobacco and Botticelli as well as they could, though most of them knew more about coal, cotton or creosote than the subjects they were affecting to discuss.

This, then, was success! To flounder helplessly in a mire of artificiality and deception to Tales of Hoffmann!

If I were asked what was the object of our going to such a dinner I could only answer that it was in order to be invited to others of the same kind. Is it for this we labor and worry—that we scheme and conspire—that we debase ourselves and lose our self-respect? Is there no wine good enough for my host? Will God let such arrogance be without a blast of fire from heaven?

* * * * *

There was a time not so very long ago when this same man was thankful enough for a slice of meat and a chunk of bread carried in a tin pail—content with the comfort of an old brier pipe filled with cut plug and smoked in a sunny corner of the factory yard. "Sunny corners of the walls of Smyrna!"

It is a fine thing to assert that here in America we have "out of a democracy of opportunity" created "an aristocracy of achievement." The phrase is stimulating and perhaps truly expresses the spirit of our energetic and ambitious country; but an aristocracy of achievement is truly noble only when the achievements themselves are fine. What are the achievements that win our applause, for which we bestow our decorations in America? Do we honor most the men who truly serve their generation and their country? Or do we fawn, rather, on those who merely serve themselves?

It is a matter of pride with us—frequently expressed in disparagement of our European contemporaries—that we are a nation of workers; that to hold any position in the community every man must have a job or otherwise lose caste; that we tolerate no loafing. We do not conceal our contempt for the chap who fails to go down every day to the office or business. Often, of course, our ostentatious workers go down, but do very little work. We feel somehow that every man owes it to the community to put in from six to ten hours' time below the residential district.

Young men who have inherited wealth are as chary of losing one hour as their clerks. The busy millionaire sits at his desk all day—his ear to the telephone. We assume that these men are useful because they are busy; but in what does their usefulness consist? What are they busy about? They are setting an example of mere industry, perhaps—but to what end? Simply, in seven cases out of ten, in order to get a few dollars or a few millions more than they have already. Their exertions have no result except to enable their families to live in even greater luxury.

I know at least fifty men, fathers of families, whose homes might radiate kindliness and sympathy and set an example of wise, generous and broad-minded living, who, already rich beyond their needs, rush downtown before their children have gone to school, pass hectic, nerve-racking days in the amassing of more money, and return after their little ones have gone to bed, too utterly exhausted to take the slightest interest in what their wives have been doing or in the pleasure and welfare of their friends.

These men doubtless give liberally to charity, but they give impersonally, not generously; they are in reality utterly selfish, engrossed in the enthralling game of becoming successful or more successful men, sacrificing their homes, their families and their health—for what? To get on; to better their position; to push in among those others who, simply because they have outstripped the rest in the matter of filling their own pockets, are hailed with acclamation.

It is pathetic to see intelligent, capable men bending their energies not to leading wholesome, well-rounded, serviceable lives but to gaining a slender foothold among those who are far less worthy of emulation than themselves and with whom they have nothing whatsoever in common except a despicable ambition to display their wealth and to demonstrate that they have "social position."

In what we call the Old World a man's social position is a matter of fixed classification—that is to say, his presumptive ability and qualifications to amuse and be amused; to hunt, fish and shoot; to ride, dance, and make himself generally agreeable—are known from the start. And, based on the premise that what is known as society exists simply for the purpose of enabling people to have a good time, there is far more reason to suppose that one who comes of a family which has made a specialty of this pursuit for several hundred years is better endowed by Nature for that purpose than one who has made a million dollars out of a patent medicine or a lucky speculation in industrial securities.

The great manufacturer or chemist in England, France, Italy, or Germany, the clever inventor, the astute banker, the successful merchant, have their due rewards; but, except in obvious instances, they are not presumed to have acquired incidentally to their material prosperity the arts of playing billiards, making love, shooting game on the wing, entertaining a house party or riding to hounds. Occasionally one of them becomes by special favor of the sovereign a baronet; but, as a rule his so-called social position is little affected by his business success, and there is no reason why it should be. He may make a fortune out of a new process, but he

42

invites the same people to dinner, frequents the same club and enjoys himself in just about the same way as he did before. His newly acquired wealth is not regarded as in itself likely to make him a more congenial dinner-table companion or any more delightful at five-o'clock tea.

The aristocracy of England and the Continent is not an aristocracy of achievement but of the polite art of killing time pleasantly. As such it has a reason for existence. Yet it can at least be said for it that its founders, however their descendants may have deteriorated, gained their original titles and positions by virtue of their services to their king and country.

However, with a strange perversity—due perhaps to our having the Declaration of Independence crammed down our throats as children—we in America seem obsessed with an ambition to create a social aristocracy, loudly proclaimed as founded on achievement, which, in point of fact, is based on nothing but the possession of money. The achievement that most certainly lands one among the crowned heads of the American nobility is admittedly the achievement of having acquired in some way or other about five million dollars; and it is immaterial whether its possessor got it by hard work, inheritance, marriage or the invention of a porous plaster.

In the wider circle of New York society are to be found a considerable number of amiable persons who have bought their position by the lavish expenditure of money amassed through the clever advertising and sale of table relishes, throat emollients, fireside novels, canned edibles, cigarettes, and chewing tobacco. The money was no doubt legitimately earned. The patent-medicine man and the millionaire tailor have my entire respect. I do not sneer at honest wealth acquired by these humble means. The rise—if it be a rise—of these and others like them is superficial evidence, perhaps, that ours is a democracy. Looking deeper, we see that it is, in fact, proof of our utter and shameless snobbery.

Most of these people are in society not on account of their personal qualities, or even by virtue of the excellence of their cut plug or throat wash which, in truth, may be a real boon to mankind—but because they have that most imperative of all necessities—money. The achievement by which they have become aristocrats is not the kind of achievement that should have entitled them to the distinction which is theirs. They are received and entertained for no other reason whatever save that they can receive and entertain in return. Their bank accounts are at the disposal of the other aristocrats—and so are their houses, automobiles and yachts. The brevet of nobility—by achievement—is conferred on them, and the American people read of their comings and goings, their balls, dinners and other festivities with consuming and reverent interest. Most dangerously significant of all is the fact that, so long as the applicant for social honors has the money, the method by which he got it, however reprehensible, is usually overlooked. That a man is a thief, so long as he has stolen enough, does not impair his desirability. The achievement of wealth is sufficient in itself to entitle him to a seat in the American House of Lords.

A substantial portion of the entertaining that takes place on Fifth Avenue is paid for out of pilfered money. Ten years ago this rhetorical remark would have been sneered at as demagogic. To-day everybody knows that it is simply the fact. Yet we continue to eat with entire unconcern the dinners that have, as it were, been abstracted from the dinner-pails of the poor. I cannot conduct an investigation into the business history of every man who asks me to his house. And even if I know he has been a crook, I cannot afford to stir up an unpleasantness by attempting in my humble way to make him feel sorrow for his misdeeds. If I did I might find myself alone— deserted by the rest of the aristocracy who are concerned less with his morality than with the vintage of his wine and the dot he is going to give his daughter.

The methods by which a newly rich American purchases a place among our nobility are simple and direct. He does not storm the inner citadel of society but at the start ingratiates himself with its lazy and easy-going outposts. He rents a house in a fashionable country suburb of New York and goes in and out of town on the "dude" train. He soon learns what professional people mingle in smart society and these he bribes to receive him and his family. He buys land and retains a "smart" lawyer to draw his deeds and attend to the transfer of title. He engages a fashionable architect to build his house, and a society young lady who has gone into landscape gardening to lay out his grounds. He cannot work the game through his dentist or plumber, but he establishes friendly relations with the swell local medical man and lets him treat an imaginary illness or two. He has his wife's portrait painted by an artist who makes a living off similar aspirants, and in exchange gets an invitation to drop in to tea at the studio. He buys broken-winded hunters from the hunting set, decrepit ponies from the polo players, and stone griffins for the garden from the social sculptress.

A couple of hundred here, a couple of thousand there, and he and his wife are dining out among the people who run things. Once he gets a foothold, the rest is by comparison easy. The bribes merely become bigger and more direct. He gives a landing to the yacht club, a silver mug for the horse show, and an altar rail to the church. He entertains wisely—gracefully discarding the doctor, lawyer, architect and artist as soon as they are no longer necessary. He has, of course, already opened an account with the fashionable broker who lives near him, and insured his life with the well-known insurance man, his neighbor. He also plays poker daily with them on the train.

This is the period during which he becomes a willing, almost eager, mark for the decayed sport who purveys bad champagne and vends his own brand of noxious cigarettes. He achieves the Stock Exchange Crowd without difficulty and moves on up into the Banking Set composed of trust company presidents, millionaires who have nothing but money, and the élite of the stockbrokers and bond men who handle their private business.

The family are by this time "going almost everywhere"; and in a year or two, if the money holds out, they can buy themselves into the inner circles. It is only necessary to take a villa at Newport and spend about one hundred thousand dollars in the course of the season. The walls of the city will fall down flat if the golden trumpet blows but mildly. And then, there they are—right in the middle of the champagne, clambakes and everything else!—invited to sit with the choicest of America's nobility on golden chairs—supplied from New York at one dollar per—and to dance to the strains of the most expensive music amid the subdued popping of distant corks.

In this social Arabian Nights' dream, however, you will find no sailors or soldiers, no great actors or writers, no real poets or artists, no genuine statesmen. The nearest you will get to any of these is the millionaire senator, or the amateur decorators and portrait painters who, by making capital of their acquaintance, get a living out of society. You will find few real people among this crowd of intellectual children.

The time has not yet come in America when a leader of smart society dares to invite to her table men and women whose only merit is that they have done something worth while. She is not sufficiently sure of her own place. She must continue all her social life to be seen only with the "right people." In England her position would be secure and she could summon whom she would to dine with her; but in New York we have to be careful lest, by asking to our houses some distinguished actor or novelist, people might think we did not know we should select our friends—not for what they are, but for what they have.

In a word, the viciousness of our social hierarchy lies in the fact that it is based solely upon material success. We have no titles of nobility; but we have Coal Barons, Merchant Princes and Kings of Finance. The very catchwords of our slang tell the story. The

45

achievement of which we boast as the foundation of our aristocracy is indeed ignoble; but, since there is no other, we and our sons, and their sons after them, will doubtless continue to struggle—and perhaps steal—to prove, to the satisfaction of ourselves and the world at large, that we are entitled to be received into the nobility of America not by virtue of our good deeds, but of our so-called success.

We would not have it otherwise. We should cry out against any serious attempt, outside of the pulpit, to alter or readjust an order that enables us to buy for money a position of which we would be otherwise undeserving. It would be most discouraging to us to have substituted for the present arrangement a society in which the only qualifications for admittance were those of charm, wit, culture, good breeding and good sportsmanship.

CHAPTER III

MY CHILDREN

I pride myself on being a man of the world—in the better sense of the phrase. I feel no regret over the passing of those romantic days when maidens swooned at the sight of a drop of blood or took refuge in the "vapors" at the approach of a strange young man; in point of fact I do not believe they ever did. I imagine that our popular idea of the fragility and sensitiveness of the weaker sex, based on the accounts of novelists of the eighteenth century, is largely a literary convention.

Heroines were endowed, as a matter of course, with the possession of all the female virtues, intensified to such a degree that they were covered with burning blushes most of the time. Languor, hysteria and general debility were regarded as the outward indications of a sweet and gentle character. Woman was a tendril clinging to the strong oak of masculinity. Modesty was her cardinal virtue. One is, of course, entitled to speculate on the probable contemporary causes for the seeming overemphasis placed on this admirable characteristic. Perhaps feminine honesty was so rare as to be at a premium and modesty was a sort of electric sign of virtue.

I am not squeamish. I have always let my children read what they would. I have never made a mystery of the relations of the sexes, for I know the call of the unseen—the fascination lent by concealment, of discovery. I believe frankness to be a good thing. A mind that is startled or shocked by the exposure of an ankle or the sight of a stocking must be essentially impure. Nor do I quarrel with woman's natural desire to adorn herself for the allurement of man. That is as inevitable as springtime.

But unquestionably the general tone of social intercourse in America, at least in fashionable centers, has recently undergone a marked and striking change. The athletic girl of the last twenty years, the girl who invited tan and freckles, wielded the tennis bat in the morning and lay basking in a bathing suit on the sand at noon, is gradually giving way to an entirely different type—a type modeled, it would seem, at least so far as dress and outward characteristics are concerned, on the French demimondaine. There are plenty of athletic girls to be found on the golf links and tennis courts; but a growing and large minority of maidens at the present time are too chary of their complexions to brave the sun. Big hats, cloudlike veils, high heels, paint and powder mark the passing of the vain hope that woman can attract the male sex by virtue of her eugenic possibilities alone.

It is but another and unpleasantly suggestive indication that the simplicity of an older generation—the rugged virtue of a more frugal time—has given place to the sophistication of the Continent. When I was a lad, going abroad was a rare and costly privilege. A youth who had been to Rome, London and Paris, and had the unusual opportunity of studying the treasures of the Vatican, the Louvre and the National Gallery, was regarded with envy. Americans went abroad for culture; to study the glories of the past.

Now the family that does not invade Europe at least every other summer is looked on as hopelessly old-fashioned. No clerk can find a job on the Rue de Rivoli or the Rue de la Paix unless he speaks fluently the dialect of the customers on whose trade his employer chiefly relies—those from Pennsylvania, New York and Illinois. The American no longer goes abroad for improvement, but to amuse himself. The college Freshman knows, at least by name, the latest beauty who haunts the Folies Bergères, and his father probably has a refined and intimate familiarity with the special attractions of Ciro's and the Trocadero.

I do not deny that we have learned valuable lessons from the Parisians. At any rate our cooking has vastly improved. Epicurus would have difficulty in choosing between the delights of New York and Paris—for, after all, New York is Paris and Paris is New York. The chef of yesterday at Voisin's rules the kitchen of the Ritz-Carlton or the Plaza to-day; and he cannot have traveled much who does not find a dozen European acquaintances among the head waiters of Broadway. Not to know Paris nowadays is felt to be as great a humiliation as it was fifty years ago not to know one's Bible.

Beyond the larger number of Americans who visit Paris for legitimate or semilegitimate purposes, there is a substantial fraction who go to do things they either cannot or dare not do at home. And as those who have not the time or the money to cross the Atlantic and who still itch for the boulevards must be kept contented, Broadway is turned into Montmartre. The result is that we cannot take our daughters to the theater without risking familiarizing them with vice in one form or another. I do not think I am overstating the situation when I say that it would be reasonably inferred from most of our so-called musical shows and farces that the natural, customary and excusable amusement of the modern man after working hours—whether the father of a family or a youth of twenty—is a promiscuous adventuring into sexual immorality.

I do not regard as particularly dangerous the vulgar French

farce where papa is caught in some extraordinary and buffoonlike situation with the washerwoman. Safety lies in exaggeration. But it is a different matter with the ordinary Broadway show, where virtue is made—at least inferentially—the object of ridicule, and sexuality is the underlying purpose of the production. During the present New York theatrical season several plays have been already censored by the authorities, and either been taken off entirely or so altered as to be still within the bounds of legal pruriency.

Whether I am right in attributing it to the influence of the French music halls or not, it is the fact that the tone of our theatergoing public is essentially low. Boys and girls who are taken in their Christmas holidays to see plays at which their parents applaud questionable songs and suggestive dances, cannot be blamed for assuming that there is not one set of morals for the stage and another for ordinary social intercourse.

Hence the college boy who has kept straight for eight months in the year is apt to wonder: What is the use? And the débutante who is curious for all the experiences her new liberty makes possible takes it for granted that an amorous trifling is the ordinary incident to masculine attention.

This is far from being mere theory. It is a matter of common knowledge that recently the most prominent restaurateur in New York found it necessary to lock up, or place a couple of uniformed maids in, every unoccupied room in his establishment whenever a private dance was given there for young people. Boys and girls of eighteen would leave these dances by dozens and, hiring taxicabs, go on slumming expeditions and excursions to the remoter corners of Central Park. In several instances parties of two or four went to the Tenderloin and had supper served in private rooms.

This is the childish expression of a demoralization that is not confined simply to smart society, but is gradually permeating the community in general. From the ordinary dinner-table conversation one hears at many of the country houses on Long Island it would be inferred that marriage was an institution of value only for legitimatizing concubinage; that an old-fashioned love affair was something to be rather ashamed of; and that morality in the young was hardly to be expected. Of course a great deal of this is mere talk and bombast, but the maid-servants hear it.

I believe, fortunately—and my belief is based on a fairly wide range of observation—that the Continental influence I have described has produced its ultimate effect chiefly among the rich; yet its operation is distinctly observable throughout American life. Nowhere is this more patent than in much of our current magazine literature and light fiction. These stories, under the guise of teaching

49

some moral lesson, are frequently designed to stimulate all the emotions that could be excited by the most vicious French novel. Some of them, of course, throw off all pretense and openly ape the petit histoire d'un amour; but essentially all are alike. The heroine is a demimondaine in everything but her alleged virtue—the hero a young bounder whose better self restrains him just in time. A conventional marriage on the last page legalizes what would otherwise have been a liaison or a degenerate flirtation.

The astonishingly unsophisticated and impossibly innocent shopgirl who—in the story—just escapes the loss of her honor; the noble young man who heroically "marries the girl"; the adventures of the debonaire actress, who turns out most surprisingly to be an angel of sweetness and light; and the Johnny whose heart is really pure gold, and who, to the reader's utter bewilderment, proves himself to be a Saint George—these are the leading characters in a great deal of our periodical literature.

A friend of mine who edits one of the more successful magazines tells me there are at least half a dozen writers who are paid guaranteed salaries of from twelve thousand dollars to eighteen thousand dollars a year for turning out each month from five thousand to ten thousand words of what is euphemistically termed "hot stuff." An erotic writer can earn yearly at the present time more than the salary of the president of the United States. What the physical result of all this is going to be does not seem to me to matter much. If the words of Jesus Christ have any significance we are already debased by our imaginations.

* * * * *

We are dangerously near an epoch of intellectual if not carnal debauchery. The prevailing tendency on the part of the young girls of to-day to imitate the dress and makeup of the Parisian cocotte is unconsciously due to this general lowering of the social moral tone. Young women in good society seem to feel that they must enter into open competition with their less fortunate sisters. And in this struggle for survival they are apparently determined to yield no advantage. Herein lies the popularity of the hobble skirt, the transparent fabric that hides nothing and follows the move of every muscle, and the otherwise senseless peculiarities and indecencies of the more extreme of the present fashions.

And here, too, is to be found the reason for the popularity of the current style of dancing, which offers no real attraction except the opportunity for a closeness of contact otherwise not permissible.

"It's all in the way it is done," says Mrs. Jones, making the customary defense. "The tango and the turkey trot can be danced as unobjectionably as the waltz."

Exactly! Only the waltz is not danced that way; and if it were the offending couple would probably be put off the floor. Moreover, their origin and history demonstrates their essentially vicious character. Is there any sensible reason why one's daughter should be encouraged to imitate the dances of the Apache and the negro debauchee? Perhaps, after all, the pendulum has merely swung just a little too far and is knocking against the case. The feet of modern progress cannot be hampered by too much of the dead underbrush of convention.

The old-fashioned prudery that in former days practically prevented rational conversation between men and women is fortunately a thing of the past, and the fact that it is no longer regarded as unbecoming for women to take an interest in all the vital problems of the day—municipal, political and hygienic— provided they can assist in their solution, marks several milestones on the highroad of advance.

On the other hand the widespread familiarity with these problems, which has been engendered simply for pecuniary profit by magazine literature in the form of essays, fiction and even verse, is by no means an undiluted blessing—particularly if the accentuation of the author is on the roses lining the path of dalliance quite as much as on the destruction to which it leads. The very warning against evil may turn out to be in effect only a hint that it is readily accessible. One does not leave the candy box open beside the baby even if the infant has received the most explicit instructions as to the probable effect of too much sugar upon its tiny kidneys. Moreover, the knowledge of the prevalence of certain vices suggests to the youthful mind that what is so universal must also be rather excusable, or at least natural.

It seems to me that, while there is at present a greater popular knowledge of the high cost of sinning, there is at the same time a greater tolerance for sin itself. Certainly this is true among the people who make up the circle of my friends. "Wild oats" are regarded as entirely a matter of course. No anecdote is too broad to be told openly at the dinner table; in point of fact the stories that used to be whispered only very discreetly in the smoking room are now told freely as the natural relishes to polite conversation. In that respect things are pretty bad.

One cannot help wondering what goes on inside the villa on Rhode Island Avenue when the eighteen-year-old daughter of the house remarks to the circle of young men and women about her at a dance: "Well, I'm going to bed—seule!" The listener furtively speculates about mama. He feels quite sure about papa. Anyhow this particular mot attracted no comment. Doubtless the young lady was as far above suspicion as the wife of Caesar; but she and her companions in this particular set have an appalling frankness of speech and a callousness in regard to discussing the more personal facts of human existence that is startling to a middle-aged man like myself.

I happened recently to overhear a bit of casual dinner-table conversation between two of the gilded ornaments of the junior set. He was a boy of twenty-five, well known for his dissipations, but, nevertheless, regarded by most mothers as a highly desirable parti.

"Oh, yes!" he remarked easily. "They asked me if I wanted to go into a bughouse, and I said I hadn't any particular objection. I was there a month. Rum place! I should worry!"

"What ward?" she inquired with polite interest.

"Inebriates', of course," said he.

I am inclined to attribute much of the questionable taste and conduct of the younger members of the fast set to neglect on the part of their mothers. Women who are busy all day and every evening with social engagements have little time to cultivate the friendship of their daughters. Hence the girl just coming out is left to shift for herself, and she soon discovers that a certain risqué freedom in manner and conversation, and a disregard of convention, will win her a superficial popularity which she is apt to mistake for success.

Totally ignorant of what she is doing or the essential character of the means she is employing, she runs wild and soon earns an unenviable reputation, which she either cannot live down or which she feels obliged to live up to in order to satisfy her craving for attention. Many a girl has gone wrong simply because she felt that it was up to her to make good her reputation for caring nothing for the proprieties.

As against an increasing looseness in talk and conduct, it is interesting to note that heavy drinking is clearly going out of fashion in smart society. There can be no question as to that. My champagne bills are not more than a third of what they were ten years ago. I do not attribute this particularly to the temperance movement. But, as against eight quarts of champagne for a dinner of twenty—which used to be about my average when we first began entertaining in New York—three are now frequently enough. I have watched the butler repeatedly at large dinner parties as he passed the wine and seen him fill only four or five glasses.

Women rarely drink at all. About one man in three takes

champagne. Of course he is apt to drink whisky instead, but by no means the same amount as formerly. If it were not for the convention requiring sherry, hock, champagne and liquors to be served the modern host could satisfy practically all the serious liquid requirements of his guests with a quart bottle of Scotch and a siphon of soda. Claret, Madeira, sparkling Moselles and Burgundies went out long ago. The fashion that has taught women self-control in eating has shown their husbands the value of abstinence. Unfortunately I do not see in this a betterment in morals, but mere self-interest—which may or may not be the same thing, according to one's philosophy. If a man drinks nowadays he drinks because he wants to and not to be a good fellow. A total abstainer finds himself perfectly at home anywhere.

Of course the fashionables, if they are going to set the pace, have to hit it up in order to head the procession. The fastness of the smart set in England is notorious, and it is the same way in France, Russia, Italy, Germany, Scandinavia—the world over; and as society tends to become unified mere national boundaries have less significance. The number of Americans who rent houses in London and Paris, and shooting boxes in Scotland, is large.

Hence the moral tone of Continental society and of the English aristocracy is gradually becoming more and more our own. But with this difference—that, as the aristocracy in England and Continental Europe is a separate caste, a well-defined order, having set metes and bounds, which considers itself superior to the rest of the population and views it with indifference, so its morals are regarded as more or less its own affair, and they do not have a wide influence on the community at large.

Even if he drinks champagne every night at dinner the Liverpool pickle merchant knows he cannot get into the king's set; but here the pickle man can not only break into the sacred circle, but he and his fat wife may themselves become the king and queen. So that a knowledge of how smart society conducts itself is an important matter to every man and woman living in the United States, since each hopes eventually to make a million dollars and move to New York. With us the fast crowd sets the example for society at large; whereas in England looseness in morals is a recognized privilege of the aristocracy to which the commoner may not aspire.

The worst feature of our situation is that the quasi-genteel working class, of whom our modern complex life supports hundreds of thousands—telephone operators, stenographers, and the like—greedily devour the newspaper accounts of the American aristocracy and model themselves, so far as possible, after it. It is almost unbelievable how intimate a knowledge these young women possess of the domestic life, manner of speech and dress of the conspicuous people in New York society.

I once stepped into the Waldorf with a friend of mine who wished to send a telephone message. He is a quiet, unassuming man of fifty, who inherited a large fortune and who is compelled, rather against his will, to do a large amount of entertaining by virtue of the position in society which Fate has thrust on him. It was a long-distance call.

"Who shall I say wants to talk?" asked the goddess with fillet-bound yellow hair in a patronizingly indifferent tone.

"Mr.—," answered my companion.

Instantly the girl's face was suffused with a smile of excited wonder.

"Are you Mr.—, the big swell who gives all the dinners and dances?" she inquired.

"I suppose I'm the man," he answered, rather amused than otherwise.

"Gee!" she cried, "ain't this luck! Look here, Mame!" she whispered hoarsely. "I've got Mr.— here on a long distance. What do you think of that!"

One cannot doubt that this telephone girl would unhesitatingly regard as above criticism anything said or done by a woman who moved in Mr.— 's circle. Unfortunately what this circle does is heralded in exaggerated terms. The influence of these partially true and often totally false reports is far-reaching and demoralizing.

The other day the young governess of a friend of my wife gave up her position, saying she was to be married. Her employer expressed an interest in the matter and asked who was going to perform the ceremony. She was surprised to learn that the functionary was to be the local country justice of the peace.

"But why aren't you going to have a clergyman marry you?" asked our friend.

"Because I don't want it too binding!" answered the girl calmly.

So far has the prevalence of divorce cast its enlightening beams.

* * * * *

I have had a shooting box in Scotland on several different occasions; and my wife has conducted successful social campaigns, as I have said before, in London, Paris, Rome and Berlin. I did not go along, but I read about it all in the papers and received weekly from the scene of conflict a pound or so of mail matter, consisting of hundreds of diaphanous sheets of paper, each covered with my daughters' fashionable humpbacked handwriting. Hastings, my stenographer, became very expert at deciphering and transcribing it on the machine for my delectation.

I was quite confused at the number and variety of the titles of nobility with which my family seemed constantly to be surrounded. They had a wonderful time, met everybody, and returned home perfected cosmopolitans. What their ethical standards are I confess I do not know exactly, for the reason that I see so little of them. They lead totally independent lives.

On rare occasions we are invited to the same houses at the same time, and on Christmas Eve we still make it a point always to stay at home together. Really I have no idea how they dispose of their time. They are always away, making visits in other cities or taking trips. They chatter fluently about literature, the theater, music, art, and know a surprising number of celebrities in this and other countries—particularly in London. They are good linguists and marvelous dancers. They are respectful, well mannered, modest, and mildly affectionate; but somehow they do not seem to belong to me. They have no troubles of which I am the confidant.

If they have any definite opinions or principles I am unaware of them; but they have the most exquisite taste. Perhaps with them this takes the place of morals. I cannot imagine my girls doing or saying anything vulgar, yet what they are like when away from home I have no means of finding out. I am quite sure that when they eventually select their husbands I shall not be consulted in the matter. My formal blessing will be all that is asked, and if that blessing is not forthcoming no doubt they will get along well enough without it.

However, I am the constant recipient of congratulations on being the parent of such charming creatures. I have succeeded— apparently—in this direction as in others. Succeeded in what? I cannot imagine these girls of mine being any particular solace to my old age.

Recently, since writing these confessions of mine, I have often wondered why my children were not more to me. I do not think they are much more to my wife. I suppose it could just as well be put the other way. Why are we not more to them? It is because, I fancy, this modern existence of ours, where every function and duty of maternity—except the actual giving of birth—is performed vicariously for us, destroys any interdependence between parents

55

and their offspring. "Smart" American mothers no longer, I am informed, nurse their babies. I know that my wife did not nurse hers. And thereafter each child had its own particular French bonne and governess besides.

Our nursery was a model of dainty comfort. All the superficial elegancies were provided for. It was a sunny, dustless apartment, with snow-white muslins, white enamel, and a frieze of grotesque Noah's Ark animals perambulating round the wall. There were huge dolls' houses, with electric lights; big closets of toys. From the earliest moment possible these three infants began to have private lessons in everything, including drawing, music and German. Their little days were as crowded with engagements then as now. Every hour was provided for; but among these multifarious occupations there was no engagement with their parents.

Even if their mother had not been overwhelmed with social duties herself my babies would, I am confident, have had no time for their parent except at serious inconvenience and a tremendous sacrifice of time. To be sure, I used occasionally to watch them decorously eating their strictly supervised suppers in the presence of the governess; but the perfect arrangements made possible by my financial success rendered parents a superfluity. They never bumped their heads, or soiled their clothes, or dirtied their little faces—so far as I knew. They never cried—at least I was never permitted to hear them.

When the time came for them to go to bed each raised a rosy little cheek and said sweetly: "Good night, papa." They had, I think, the usual children's diseases—exactly which ones I am not sure of; but they had them in the hospital room at the top of the house, from which I was excluded, and the diseases progressed with medical propriety in due course and under the efficient management of starchy trained nurses.

Their outdoor life consisted in walking the asphalt pavements of Central Park, varied with occasional visits to the roller-skating rink; but their social life began at the age of four or five. I remember these functions vividly, because they were so different from those of my own childhood. The first of these was when my eldest daughter attained the age of six years. Similar events in my private history had been characterized by violent games of blind man's buff, hide and seek, hunt the slipper, going to Jerusalem, ring-round-a-rosy, and so on, followed by a dish of ice-cream and hairpulling.

Not so with my offspring. Ten little ladies and gentlemen, accompanied by their maids, having been rearranged in the dressing room downstairs, were received by my daughter with due form in the drawing room. They were all flounced, ruffled and beribboned. Two little boys of seven had on Eton suits. Their behavior was impeccable.

Almost immediately a professor of legerdemain made his appearance and, with the customary facility of his brotherhood, proceeded to remove tons of débris from presumably empty hats, rabbits from handkerchiefs, and hard-boiled eggs from childish noses and ears. The assembled group watched him with polite tolerance. At intervals there was a squeal of surprise, but it soon developed that most of them had already seen the same trickman half a dozen times. However, they kindly consented to be amused, and the professor gave way to a Punch and Judy show of a sublimated variety, which the youthful audience viewed with mild approval.

The entertainment concluded with a stereopticon exhibition of supposedly humorous events, which obviously did not strike the children as funny at all. Supper was laid in the dining room, where the table had been arranged as if for a banquet of diplomats. There were flowers in abundance and a life-size swan of icing at each end. Each child was assisted by its own nurse, and our butler and a footman served, in stolid dignity, a meal consisting of rice pudding, cereals, cocoa, bread and butter, and ice-cream.

It was by all odds the most decorous affair ever held in our house. At the end the gifts were distributed—Parisian dolls, toy baby-carriages and paint boxes for the girls; steam engines, magic lanterns and miniature circuses for the boys. My bill for these trifles came to one hundred and twelve dollars. At half-past six the carriages arrived and our guests were hurried away.

I instance this affair because it struck the note of elegant propriety that has always been the tone of our family and social life. The children invited to the party were the little boys and girls whose fathers and mothers we thought most likely to advance their social interests later on.

Of these children two of the girls have married members of the foreign nobility—one a jaded English lord, the other a worthless and dissipated French count; another married—fifteen years later—one of these same little boys and divorced him within eighteen months; while two of the girls—our own—have not married.

Of the boys one wedded an actress; another lives in Paris and studies "art"; one has been already accounted for; and two have given their lives to playing polo, the stock market, and elevating the chorus.

Beginning at this early period, my two daughters, and later on my son, met only the most select young people of their own age in New York and on Long Island. I remember being surprised at the amount of theatergoing they did by the time the eldest was nine years old. My wife made a practice of giving a children's theater party every Saturday and taking her small guests to the matinée. As the theaters were more limited in number then than now these comparative infants sooner or later saw practically everything that was on the boards—good, bad and indifferent; and they displayed a precocity of criticism that quite astounded me.

Their real social career began with children's dinners and dancing parties by the time they were twelve, and their later coming out changed little the mode of life to which they had been accustomed for several years before it. The result of their mother's watchful care and self-sacrifice is that these two young ladies could not possibly be happy, or even comfortable, if they married men unable to furnish them with French maids, motors, constant amusement, gay society, travel and Paris clothes.

Without these things they would wither away and die like flowers deprived of the sun. They are physically unfit to be anything but the wives of millionaires—and they will be the wives of millionaires or assuredly die unmarried. But, as the circle of rich young men of their acquaintance is more or less limited their chances of matrimony are by no means bright, albeit that they are the pivots of a furious whirl of gaiety which never stops.

No young man with an income of less than twenty thousand a year would have the temerity to propose to either of them. Even on twenty thousand they would have a hard struggle to get along; it would mean the most rigid economy—and, if there were babies, almost poverty.

Besides, when girls are living in the luxury to which mine are accustomed they think twice before essaying matrimony at all. The prospects of changing Newport, Palm Beach, Paris, Rome, Nice and Biarritz for the privilege of bearing children in a New York apartment house does not allure, as in the case of less cosmopolitan young ladies. There must be love—plus all present advantages! Present advantages withdrawn, love becomes cautious.

Even though the rich girl herself is of finer clay than her parents and, in spite of her artificial environment and the false standards by which she is surrounded, would like to meet and perhaps eventually marry some young man who is more worth while than the "pet cats" of her acquaintance, she is practically powerless to do so. She is cut off by the impenetrable artificial barrier of her own exclusiveness. She may hear of such young men—young fellows of ambition, of adventurous spirit, of genius, who have already achieved something in the world, but they are outside the wall of money and she is inside it, and there is no way for them to get in or for her to get out. She is permitted to know only the jeunesse dorée—the fops, the sports, the club-window men, whose antecedents are vouched for by the Social Register.

She has no way of meeting others. She does not know what the others are like. She is only aware of an instinctive distaste for most of the young fellows among whom she is thrown. At best they are merely innocuous when they are not offensive. They do nothing; they intend never to do anything. If she is the American girl of our plays and novels she wants something better; and in the plays and novels she always gets him—the dashing young ranchman, the heroic naval lieutenant, the fearless Alaskan explorer, the tireless prospector or daring civil engineer. But in real life she does not get him—except by the merest fluke of fortune. She does not know the real thing when she meets it, and she is just as likely to marry a dissipated groom or chauffeur as the young Stanley of her dreams.

The saddest class in our social life is that of the thoroughbred American girl who is a thousand times too good for her de-luxe surroundings and the crew of vacuous la-de-da Willies hanging about her, yet who, absolutely cut off from contact with any others, either gradually fades into a peripatetic old maid, wandering over Europe, or marries an eligible, turkey-trotting nondescript—"a mimmini-pimmini, Francesca da Rimini, je-ne-sais-quoi young man."

The Atlantic seaboard swarms in summertime with broad-shouldered, well-bred, highly educated and charming boys, who have had every advantage except that of being waited on by liveried footmen. They camp in the woods; tutor the feeble-minded sons of the rich; tramp and bicycle over Swiss mountain passes; sail their catboats through the island-studded reaches and thoroughfares of the Maine coast, and grow brown and hard under the burning sun. They are the hope of America. They can carry a canoe or a hundred-pound pack over a forest trail; and in the winter they set the pace in the scientific, law and medical schools. Their heads are clear, their eyes are bright, and there is a hollow instead of a bow window beneath the buttons of their waistcoats.

The feet of these young men carry them to strange places; they cope with many and strange monsters. They are our Knights of the Round Table. They find the Grail of Achievement in lives of hard work, simple pleasures and high ideals—in college and factory towns; in law courts and hospitals; in the mountains of Colorado and the plains of the Dakotas. They are the best we have; but the poor rich girl rarely, if ever, meets them. The barrier of wealth completely hems her in. She must take one of those inside or nothing.

When, in a desperate revolt against the artificiality of her existence, she breaks through the wall she is easy game for anybody—as likely to marry a jockey or a professional forger as one of the young men of her desire. One should not blame a rich girl too much for marrying a titled and perhaps attractive foreigner. The would-be critic has only to step into a Fifth Avenue ballroom and see what she is offered in his place to sympathize with and perhaps applaud her selection. Better a year of Europe than a cycle of—shall we say, Narragansett? After all, why not take the real thing, such as it is, instead of an imitation?

I believe that one of the most cruel results of modern social life is the cutting off of young girls from acquaintanceship with youths of the sturdy, intelligent and hardworking type—and the unfitting of such girls for anything except the marriage mart of the millionaire.

I would give half of all I possess to see my daughters happily married; but I now realize that their education renders such a marriage highly difficult of satisfactory achievement. Their mother and I have honestly tried to bring them up in such a way that they can do their duty in that state of life to which it hath pleased God to call them. But unfortunately, unless some man happens to call them also, they will have to keep on going round and round as they are going now.

We did not anticipate the possibility of their becoming old maids, and they cannot become brides of the church. I should honestly be glad to have either of them marry almost anybody, provided he is a decent fellow. I should not even object to their marrying foreigners, but the difficulty is that it is almost impossible to find out whether a foreigner is really decent or not. It is true that the number of foreign noblemen who marry American girls for love is negligible. There is undoubtedly a small and distinguished minority who do so; but the transaction is usually a matter of bargain and sale, and the man regards himself as having lived up to his contract by merely conferring his title on the woman he thus deigns to honor.

I should prefer to have them marry Americans, of course; but I no longer wish them to marry Americans of their own class. Yet, unfortunately, they would be unwilling to marry out of it. A curious situation! I have given up my life to buying a place for my children that is supposed to give them certain privileges, and I now am loath to have them take advantage of those privileges.

The situation has its amusing as well as its pathetic side—for my son, now that I come to think of it, is one of the eligibles. He knows everybody and is on the road to money. He is one of the opportunities that society is offering to the daughters of other successful men. Should I wish my own girls to marry a youth like him? Far from it! Yet he is exactly the kind of fellow that my success has enabled them to meet and know, and whom Fate decrees that they shall eventually marry if they marry at all.

When I frankly face the question of how much happiness I get out of my children I am constrained to admit that it is very little. The sense of proprietorship in three such finished products is something, to be sure; and, after all, I suppose they have—concealed somewhere—a real affection for their old dad. At times they are facetious—almost playful—as on my birthday; but I fancy that arises from a feeling of embarrassment at not knowing how to be intimate with a parent who crosses their path only twice a week, and then on the stairs.

My son has attended to his own career now for some fourteen years; in fact I lost him completely before he was out of knickerbockers. Up to the time when he was sent away to boarding school he spent a rather disconsolate childhood, playing with mechanical toys, roller skating in the Mall, going occasionally to the theater, and taking music lessons; but he showed so plainly the debilitating effect of life in the city for eight months in the year that at twelve he was bundled off to a country school. Since then he has grown to manhood without our assistance. He went away undersized, pale, with a meager little neck and a sort of wistful Nicholas Nickelby expression. When he returned at the Christmas vacation he had gained ten pounds, was brown and freckled, and looked like a small giraffe in pantalets.

Moreover, he had entirely lost the power of speech, owing to a fear of making a fool of himself. During the vacation in question he was reoutfitted and sent three times a week to the theater. On one or two occasions I endeavored to ascertain how he liked school, but all I could get out of him was the vague admission that it was "all right" and that he liked it "well enough." This process of outgrowing his clothes and being put through a course of theaters at each vacation—there was nothing else to do with him—continued for seven years, during which time he grew to be six feet two inches in height and gradually filled out to man's size. He managed to hold a place in the lower third of his class, with the aid of constant and expensive tutoring in the summer vacations, and he finally was graduated with the rest and went to Harvard.

By this time he preferred to enjoy himself in his own way during his leisure and we saw less of him than ever. But, whatever his intellectual achievements may be, there is no doubt as to his being a man of the world, entirely at ease anywhere, with perfect manners and all the social graces. I do not think he was particularly dissipated at Harvard; on the other hand, I am assured by the dean that he was no student. He "made" a select club early in his course and from that time was occupied, I suspect, in playing poker and bridge, discussing deep philosophical questions and acquiring the art of living. He never went in for athletics; but by doing nothing in a highly artistic manner, and by dancing with the most startling agility, he became a prominent social figure and a headliner in college theatricals.

From his sophomore year he has been in constant demand for cotillions, house parties and yachting trips. His intimate pals seem to be middle-aged millionaires who are known to me in only the most casual way; and he is a sort of gentleman-in-waiting—I believe the accepted term is "pet cat"—to several society women, for whom he devises new cotillion figures, arranges original after-dinner entertainments and makes himself generally useful.

Like my two daughters he has arrived—absolutely; but, though we are members of the same learned profession, he is almost a stranger to me. I had no difficulty in getting him a clerkship in a gilt-edged law firm immediately after he was admitted to the bar and he is apparently doing marvelously well, though what he can possibly know of law will always remain a mystery to me. Yet he is already, at the age of twenty-eight, a director in three important concerns whose securities are listed on the stock exchange, and he spends a great deal of money, which he must gather somehow. I know that his allowance cannot do much more than meet his accounts at the smart clubs to which he belongs.

He is a pleasant fellow and I enjoy the rare occasions when I catch a glimpse of him. I do not think he has any conspicuous vices—or virtues. He has simply had sense enough to take advantage of his social opportunities and bids fair to be equally successful with myself. He has really never done a stroke of work in his life, but has managed to make himself agreeable to those who could help him along. I have no doubt those rich friends of his throw enough business in his way to net him ten or fifteen thousand dollars a year, but I should hesitate to retain him to defend me if I were arrested for speeding.

Nevertheless at dinner I have seen him bullyrag and browbeat a judge of our Supreme Court in a way that made me shudder, though I admit that the judge in question owed his appointment entirely to the friend of my son who happened to be giving the dinner; and he will contradict in a loud tone men and women older than myself, no matter what happens to be the subject under discussion. They seem to like it—why, I do not pretend to understand. They admire his assurance and good nature, and are rather afraid of him!

I cannot imagine what he would find to do in my own law office; he would doubtless regard it as a dull place and too narrow a sphere for his splendid capabilities. He is a clever chap, this son of mine; and though neither he nor his sisters seem to have any particular fondness for one another, he is astute at playing into their hands and they into his. He also keeps a watchful eye on our dinner invitations, so they will not fall below the properly exclusive standard.

"What are you asking old Washburn for?" he will ask. "He's been a dead one these five years!" Or: "I'd cut out the Becketts—at least if you're asking the Thompsons. They don't go with the same crowd." Or: "Why don't you ask the Peyton-Smiths? They're nothing to be afraid of if they do cut a dash at Newport. The old girl is rather a pal of mine."

So we drop old Washburn, cut out the Becketts, and take courage and invite the hyphenated Smiths. A hint from him pays handsome dividends! and he is distinctly proud of the family and anxious to push it along to still greater success.

However, he has never asked my help or assistance—except in a financial way. He has never come to me for advice; never confided any of his perplexities or troubles to me. Perhaps he has none. He seems quite sufficient unto himself. And he certainly is not my friend. It seems strange that these three children of mine, whose upbringing has been the source of so much thought and planning on the part of my wife and myself, and for whose ultimate benefit we have shaped our own lives, should be the merest, almost impersonal, acquaintances.

The Italian fruit-vender on the corner, whose dirty offspring crawl among the empty barrels behind the stand, knows far more of his children than do we of ours, will have far more influence on the shaping of their future lives. They do not need us now and they never have needed us. A trust company could have performed all the offices of parenthood with which we have been burdened. We have paid others to be father and mother in our stead—or rather, as I now see, have had hired servants to go through the motions for us;

63

and they have done it well, so far as the mere physical side of the matter is concerned. We have been almost entirely relieved of care.

We have never been annoyed by our children's presence at any time. We have never been bothered with them at meals. We have never had to sit up with them when they could not go to sleep, or watch at their bedsides during the night when they were sick. Competent nurses—far more competent than we—washed their little dirty hands, mended the torn dresses and kissed their wounds to make them well. And when five o'clock came three dainty little Dresden figures in pink and blue ribbons were brought down to the drawing room to be admired by our guests. Then, after being paraded, they were carried back to the nursery to resume the even tenor of their independent existences.

No one of us has ever needed the other members of the family. My wife has never called on either of our daughters to perform any of those trifling intimate services that bring a mother and her children together. There has always been a maid standing ready to hook up her dress, fetch her book or her hat, or a footman to spring upstairs after the forgotten gloves. And the girls have never needed their mother—the governess could read aloud ever so much better, and they always had their own maid to look after their clothes. When they needed new gowns they simply went downtown and bought them—and the bill was sent to my office. Neither of them was ever forced to stay at home that her sister might have some pleasure instead. No; our wealth has made it possible for each of my children to enjoy every luxury without any sacrifice on another's part. They owe nothing to each other, and they really owe nothing to their mother or myself—except perhaps a monetary obligation.

But there is one person, technically not one of our family, for whom my girls have the deepest and most sincere affection—that is old Jane, their Irish nurse, who came to them just after they were weaned and stayed with us until the period of maids and governesses arrived. I paid her twenty-five dollars a month, and for nearly ten years she never let them out of her sight—crooning over them at night; trudging after them during the daytime; mending their clothes; brushing their teeth; cutting their nails; and teaching them strange Irish legends of the banshee. When I called her into the library and told her the children were now too old for her and that they must have a governess, the look that came into her face haunted me for days.

"Ye'll be after taking my darlin's away from me?" she muttered in a dead tone. "'T will be hard for me!" She stood as if the heart had died within her, and the hundred-dollar bill I shoved into her hand fell to the floor. Then she turned quickly and hurried out of the room without a sob. I heard afterward that she cried for a week.

Now I always know when one of their birthdays has arrived by the queer package, addressed in old Jane's quaint half-printed writing, that always comes. She has cared for many dozens of children since then, but loves none like my girls, for she came to them in her young womanhood and they were her first charges.

And they are just as fond of her. Indeed it is their loyalty to this old Irish nurse that gives me faith that they are not the cold propositions they sometimes seem to be. For once when, after much careless delay, a fragmentary message came to us that she was ill and in a hospital my two daughters, who were just starting for a ball, flew to her bedside, sat with her all through the night and never left her until she was out of danger.

"They brought me back—my darlin's!" she whispered to us when later we called to see how she was getting on; and my wife looked at me across the rumpled cot and her lips trembled. I knew what was in her mind. Would her daughters have rushed to her with the same forgetfulness of self as to this prematurely gray and wrinkled woman whose shrunken form lay between us?

Poor old Jane! Alone in an alien land, giving your life and your love to the children of others, only to have them torn from your arms just as the tiny fingers have entwined themselves like tendrils round your heart! We have tossed you the choicest blessings of our lives and shouldered you with the heavy responsibilities that should rightfully have been our load. Your cup has run over with both joy and sorrow but you have drunk of the cup, while we are still thirsty! Our hearts are dry, while yours is green—nourished with the love that should belong to us. Poor old Jane? Lucky old Jane! Anyhow God bless you!

CHAPTER IV

MY MIND

I come of a family that prides itself on its culture and intellectuality. We have always been professional people, for my grandfather was, as I have said, a clergyman; and among my uncles are a lawyer, a physician and a professor. My sisters, also, have intermarried with professional men. I received a fairly good primary and secondary education, and graduated from my university with honors—whatever that may have meant. I was distinctly of a literary turn of mind; and during my four years of study I imbibed some slight information concerning the English classics, music, modern history and metaphysics. I could talk quite wisely about Chaucer, Beaumont and Fletcher, Thomas Love Peacock and Ann Radcliffe, or Kant, Fichte and Schopenhauer.

I can see now that my smattering of culture was neither deep nor broad. I acquired no definite knowledge of underlying principles, of general history, of economics, of languages, of mathematics, of physics or of chemistry. To biology and its allies I paid scarcely any attention at all, except to take a few snap courses. I really secured only a surface acquaintance with polite English literature, mostly very modern. The main part of my time I spent reading Stevenson and Kipling. I did well in English composition and I pronounced my words neatly and in a refined manner. At the end of my course, when twenty-two years old, I was handed an imitation-parchment degree and proclaimed by the president of the college as belonging to the Brotherhood of Educated Men.

I did not. I was an imitation educated man; but, though spurious, I was a sufficiently good counterfeit to pass current for what I had been declared to be. Apart from a little Latin, a considerable training in writing the English language, and a great deal of miscellaneous reading of an extremely light variety, I really had no culture at all. I could not speak an idiomatic sentence in French or German; I had the vaguest ideas about applied mechanics and science; and no thorough knowledge about anything; but I was supposed to be an educated man, and on this stock in trade I have done business ever since—with, to be sure, the added capital of a degree of bachelor of laws.

Now since my graduation, twenty-eight years ago, I have given no time to the systematic study of any subject except law. I

66

have read no serious works dealing with either history, sociology, economics, art or philosophy. I am supposed to know enough about these subjects already. I have rarely read over again any of the masterpieces of English literature with which I had at least a bowing acquaintance when at college. Even this last sentence I must qualify to the extent of admitting that I now see that this acquaintance was largely vicarious, and that I frequently read more criticism than literature.

It is characteristic of modern education that it is satisfied with the semblance and not the substance of learning. I was taught about Shakspere, but not Shakspere. I was instructed in the history of literature, but not in literature itself. I knew the names of the works of numerous English authors and I knew what Taine and others thought about them, but I knew comparatively little of what was between the covers of the books themselves. I was, I find, a student of letters by proxy. As time went on I gradually forgot that I had not, in fact, actually perused these volumes; and to-day I am accustomed to refer familiarly to works I never have read at all—not a difficult task in these days of handbook knowledge and literary varnish.

It is this patent superficiality that so bores me with the affected culture of modern social intercourse. We all constantly attempt to discuss abstruse subjects in philosophy and art, and pretend to a familiarity with minor historical characters and events. Now why try to talk about Bergson's theories if you have not the most elementary knowledge of philosophy or metaphysics? Or why attempt to analyze the success or failure of a modern post-impressionist painter when you are totally ignorant of the principles of perspective or of the complex problems of light and shade? You might as properly presume to discuss a mastoid operation with a surgeon or the doctrine of cypres with a lawyer. You are equally qualified.

I frankly confess that my own ignorance is abysmal. In the last twenty-eight years what information I have acquired has been picked up principally from newspapers and magazines; yet my library table is littered with books on modern art and philosophy, and with essays on literary and historical subjects. I do not read them. They are my intellectual window dressings. I talk about them with others who, I suspect, have not read them either; and we confine ourselves to generalities, with a careful qualification of all expressed opinions, no matter how vague and elusive. For example—a safe conversational opening:

"Of course there is a great deal to be said in favor of Bergson's general point of view, but to me his reasoning is inconclusive. Don't you feel the same way—somehow?"

You can try this on almost anybody. It will work in ninety-nine cases out of a hundred; for, of course, there is a great deal to be said in favor of the views of anybody who is not an absolute fool, and most reasoning is open to attack at least for being inconclusive. It is also inevitable that your cultured friend—or acquaintance—should feel the same way—somehow. Most people do—in a way.

The real truth of the matter is, all I know about Bergson is that he is a Frenchman—is he actually by birth a Frenchman or a Belgian?—who as a philosopher has a great reputation on the Continent, and who recently visited America to deliver some lectures. I have not the faintest idea what his theories are, and I should not if I heard him explain them. Moreover, I cannot discuss philosophy or metaphysics intelligently, because I have not to-day the rudimentary knowledge necessary to understand what it is all about.

It is the same with art. On the one or two isolated varnishing days when we go to a gallery we criticize the pictures quite fiercely. "We know what we like." Yes, perhaps we do. I am not sure even of that. But in eighty-five cases out of a hundred none of us have any knowledge of the history of painting or any intelligent idea of why Velasquez is regarded as a master; yet we acquire a glib familiarity with the names of half a dozen cubists or futurists, and bandy them about much as my office boy does the names of his favorite pugilists or baseball players.

It is even worse with history and biography. We cannot afford or have not the decency to admit that we are uninformed. We speak casually of, say, Henry of Navarre, or Beatrice D'Este, or Charles the Fifth. I select my names intentionally from among the most celebrated in history; yet how many of us know within two hundred years of when any one of them lived—or much about them? How much definite historical information have we, even about matters of genuine importance?

* * * * *

Let us take a shot at a few dates. I will make it childishly easy. Give me, if you can, even approximately, the year of Caesar's Conquest of Gaul; the Invasion of Europe by the Huns; the Sack of Rome; the Battle of Châlons-sur-Marne; the Battle of Tours; the Crowning of Charlemagne; the Great Crusade; the Fall of Constantinople; Magna Charta; the Battle of Crécy; the Field of the Cloth of Gold; the Massacre of St. Bartholomew; the Spanish Armada; the Execution of King Charles I; the Fall of the Bastile; the

Inauguration of George Washington; the Battle of Waterloo; the Louisiana Purchase; the Indian Mutiny; the Siege of Paris.

I will look out of the window while you go through the mental agony of trying to remember. It looks easy, does it not? Almost an affront to ask the date of Waterloo! Well, I wanted to be fair and even things up; but, honestly, can you answer correctly five out of these twenty elementary questions? I doubt it. Yet you have, no doubt, lying on your table at the present time, intimate studies of past happenings and persons that presuppose and demand a rough general knowledge of American, French or English history.

The dean of Radcliffe College, who happened to be sitting behind two of her recent graduates while attending a performance of Parker's deservedly popular play "Disraeli" last winter, overheard one of them say to the other: "You know, I couldn't remember whether Disraeli was in the Old or the New Testament; and I looked in both and couldn't find him in either!"

I still pass socially as an exceptionally cultured man—one who is well up on these things; yet I confess to knowing to-day absolutely nothing of history, either ancient, medieval or modern. It is not a matter of mere dates, by any means, though I believe dates to be of some general importance. My ignorance is deeper than that. I do not remember the events themselves or their significance. I do not now recall any of the facts connected with the great epoch-making events of classic times; I cannot tell as I write, for example, who fought in the battle of the Allia; why Caesar crossed the Rubicon, or why Cicero delivered an oration against Catiline.

As to what subsequently happened on the Italian peninsula my mind is a blank until the appearance of Garibaldi during the last century. I really never knew just who Garibaldi was until I read Trevelyan's three books on the Resorgimento last winter, and those I perused because I had taken a motor trip through Italy the summer before. I know practically nothing of Spanish history, and my mind is a blank as to Russia, Poland, Turkey, Sweden, Germany, Austria, and Holland.

Of course I know that the Dutch Republic rose—assisted by one Motley, of Boston—and that William of Orange was a Hollander—or at least I suppose he was born there. But how Holland came to rise I know not—or whether William was named after an orange or oranges were named after him.

As for central Europe, it is a shocking fact that I never knew there was not some interdependency between Austria and Germany until last summer. I only found out the contrary when I started to motor through the Austrian Tyrol and was held up by the custom officers on the frontier. I knew that an old emperor named William

69

somehow founded the German Empire out of little states, with the aid of Bismarck and Von Moltke; but that is all I know about it. I do not know when the war between Prussia and Austria took place or what battles were fought in it.

The only battle in the Franco-Prussian War I am sure of is Sedan, which I remember because I was once told that Phil Sheridan was present as a spectator. I know Gustavus Adolphus was a king of Sweden, but I do not know when; and apart from their names I know nothing of Theodoric, Charles Martel, Peter the Hermit, Lodovico Moro, the Emperor Maximilian, Catherine of Aragon, Catherine de' Medici, Richelieu, Frederick Barbarossa, Cardinal Wolsey, Prince Rupert—I do not refer to Anthony Hope's hero, Rupert of Hentzau—Saint Louis, Admiral Coligny, or the thousands of other illustrious personages that crowd the pages of history.

I do not know when or why the Seven Years' War, the Thirty Years' War, the Hundred Years' War or the Massacre of St. Bartholomew took place, why the Edict of Nantes was revoked or what it was, or who fought at Malplaquet, Tours, Soissons, Marengo, Plassey, Oudenarde, Fontenoy or Borodino—or when they occurred. I probably did know most if not all of these things, but I have entirely forgotten them. Unfortunately I manage to act as if I had not. The result is that, having no foundation to build on, any information I do acquire is immediately swept away. People are constantly giving me books on special topics, such as Horace Walpole and his Friends, France in the Thirteenth Century, The Holland House Circle, or Memoires of Madame du Barry; but of what use can they be to me when I do not know, or at least have forgotten, even the salient facts of French and English history?

We are undoubtedly the most superficial people in the world about matters of this sort. Any bluff goes. I recall being at a dinner not long ago when somebody mentioned Conrad II. One of the guests hazarded the opinion that he had died in the year 1330. This would undoubtedly have passed muster but for a learned-looking person farther down the table who deprecatingly remarked: "I do not like to correct you, but I think Conrad the Second died in 1337!" The impression created on the assembled company cannot be overstated. Later on in the smoking room I ventured to compliment the gentleman on his fund of information, saying:

"Why, I never even heard of Conrad the Second!"

"Nor I either," he answered shamelessly.

It is the same with everything—music, poetry, politics. I go night after night to hear the best music in the world given at fabulous cost in the Metropolitan Opera House and am content to murmur vague ecstasies over Caruso, without being aware of who wrote the opera or what it is all about. Most of us know nothing of orchestration or even the names of the different instruments. We may not even be sure of what is meant by counterpoint or the difference between a fugue and an arpeggio.

A handbook would give us these minor details in an hour's reading; but we prefer to sit vacuously making feeble jokes about the singers or the occupants of the neighboring boxes, without a single intelligent thought as to why the composer attempted to write precisely this sort of an opera, when he did it, or how far he succeeded. We are content to take our opinions and criticisms ready made, no matter from whose mouth they fall; and one hears everywhere phrases that, once let loose from the Pandora's Box of some foolish brain, never cease from troubling.

In science I am in even a more parlous state. I know nothing of applied electricity in its simplest forms. I could not explain the theory of the gas engine, and plumbing is to me one of the great mysteries.

Last, but even more lamentable, I really know nothing about politics, though I am rather a strong party man and my name always appears on important citizens' committees about election time. I do not know anything about the city departments or its fiscal administration. I should not have the remotest idea where to direct a poor person who applied to me for relief. Neither have I ever taken the trouble to familiarize myself with even the more important city buildings.

Of course I know the City Hall by sight, but I have never been inside it; I have never visited the Tombs or any one of our criminal courts; I have never been in a police station, a fire house, or inspected a single one of our prisons or reformatory institutions. I do not know whether police magistrates are elected or appointed and I could not tell you in what congressional district I reside. I do not know the name of my alderman, assemblyman, state senator or representative in Congress.

I do not know who is at the head of the Fire Department, the Street Cleaning Department, the Health Department, the Park Department or the Water Department; and I could not tell, except for the Police Department, what other departments there are. Even so, I do not know what police precinct I am living in, the name of the captain in command, or where the nearest fixed post is at which an officer is supposed to be on duty.

As I write I can name only five members of the United States Supreme Court, three members of the Cabinet, and only one of the congressmen from the state of New York. This in cold type seems almost preposterous, but it is, nevertheless, a fact—and I am an active practicing lawyer besides. I am shocked to realize these things. Yet I am supposed to be an exceptionally intelligent member of the community and my opinion is frequently sought on questions of municipal politics.

Needless to say, the same indifference has prevented my studying—except in the most superficial manner—the single tax, free trade and protection, the minimum wage, the recall, referendum, or any other of the present much-mooted questions. How is this possible? The only answer I can give is that I have confined my mental activities entirely to making my legal practice as lucrative as possible. I have taken things as I found them and put up with abuses rather than go to the trouble to do away with them. I have no leisure to try to reform the universe. I leave that task to others whose time is less valuable than mine and who have something to gain by getting into the public eye.

The mere fact, however, that I am not interested in local politics would not ordinarily, in a normal state of civilization, explain my ignorance of these things. In most societies they would be the usual subjects of conversation. People naturally discuss what interests them most. Uneducated people talk about the weather, their work, their ailments and their domestic affairs. With more enlightened folk the conversation turns on broader topics—the state of the country, politics, trade, or art.

It is only among the so-called society people that the subjects selected for discussion do not interest anybody. Usually the talk that goes on at dinners or other entertainments relates only to what plays the conversationalists in question have seen or which of the best sellers they have read. For the rest the conversation is dexterously devoted to the avoidance of the disclosure of ignorance. Even among those who would like to discuss the questions of the day intelligently and to ascertain other people's views pertaining to them, there is such a fundamental lack of elementary information that it is a hopeless undertaking. They are reduced to the commonplaces of vulgar and superficial comment.

"'Tis plain," cry they, "our mayor's a noddy; and as for the corporation—shocking!"

The mayor may be and probably is a noddy, but his critics do not know why. The average woman who dines out hardly knows what she is saying or what is being said to her. She will usually agree with any proposition that is put to her—if she has heard it. Generally she does not listen.

I know a minister's wife who never pays the slightest attention to anything that is being said to her, being engrossed in a torrent of explanation regarding her children's education and minor diseases. Once a bored companion in a momentary pause fixed her sternly with his eye and said distinctly: "But I don't give a—- about your children!" At which the lady smiled brightly and replied: "Yes. Quite so. Exactly! As I was saying, Johnny got a—"

But, apart from such hectic people, who run quite amuck whenever they open their mouths, there are large numbers of men and women of some intelligence who never make the effort to express conscientiously any ideas or opinions. They find it irksome to think. They are completely indifferent as to whether a play is really good or bad or who is elected mayor of the city. In any event they will have their coffee, rolls and honey served in bed the next morning; and they know that, come what will—flood, tempest, fire or famine—there will be forty-six quarts of extra xxx milk left at their area door. They are secure. The stock market may rise and fall, presidents come and go, but they will remain safe in the security of fifty thousand a year. And, since they really do not care about anything, they are as likely to praise as to blame, and to agree with everybody about everything. Their world is all cakes and ale—why should they bother as to whether the pothouse beer is bad?

I confess, with something of a shock, that essentially I am like the rest of these people. The reason I am not interested in my country and my city is because, by reason of my financial and social independence, they have ceased to be my city and country. I should be just as comfortable if our Government were a monarchy. It really is nothing to me whether my tax rate is six one-hundredths of one per cent higher or lower, or what mayor rules in City Hall.

So long as Fifth Avenue is decently paved, so that my motor runs smoothly when I go to the opera, I do not care whether we have a Reform, Tammany or Republican administration in the city. So far as I am concerned, my valet will still come into my bedroom at exactly nine o'clock every morning, turn on the heat and pull back the curtains. His low, modulated "Your bath is ready, sir," will steal through my dreams, and he will assist me to rise and put on my embroidered dressing gown of wadded silk in preparation for another day's hard labor in the service of my fellowmen. Times have changed since my father's frugal college days. Have they changed for better or for worse?

Of one thing I am certain—my father was a better-educated man than I am. I admit that, under the circumstances, this does not imply very much; but my parent had, at least, some solid ground beneath his intellectual feet on which he could stand. His mind was thoroughly disciplined by rigid application to certain serious studies that were not selected by himself. From the day he entered college he was in active competition with his classmates in all his studies, and if he had been a shirker they would all have known it.

In my own case, after I had once matriculated, the elective system left me free to choose my own subjects and to pursue them faithfully or not, so long as I could manage to squeak through my examinations. My friends were not necessarily among those who elected the same courses, and whether I did well or ill was nobody's business but my own and the dean's. It was all very pleasant and exceedingly lackadaisical, and by the time I graduated I had lost whatever power of concentration I had acquired in my preparatory schooling. At the law school I was at an obvious disadvantage with the men from the smaller colleges which still followed the old-fashioned curriculum and insisted on the mental discipline entailed by advanced Greek, Latin, the higher mathematics, science and biology.

In point of fact I loafed delightfully for four years and let my mind run absolutely to seed, while I smoked pipe after pipe under the elms, watching the squirrels and dreaming dreams. I selected elementary—almost childlike—courses in a large variety of subjects; and as soon as I had progressed sufficiently to find them difficult I cast about for other snaps to take their places. My bookcase exhibited a collection of primers on botany, zoölogy and geology, the fine arts, music, elementary French and German, philosophy, ethics, methaphysics, architecture, English composition, Shakspere, the English poets and novelists, oral debating and modern history.

I took nothing that was not easy and about which I did not already know a little something. I attended the minimum number of lectures required, did the smallest amount of reading possible and, by cramming vigorously for three weeks at the end of the year, managed to pass all examinations creditably. I averaged, I suppose, outside of the lecture room, about a single hour's desultory work a day. I really need not have done that.

When, for example, it came time to take the examination in French composition I discovered that I had read but two out of the fifteen plays and novels required, the plots of any one of which I might be asked to give on my paper. Rather than read these various volumes, I prepared a skeleton digest in French, sufficiently vague, which could by slight transpositions be made to do service in every case. I committed it to memory. It ran somewhat as follows:

"The play"—or novel—"entitled— is generally conceded to be one of the most carefully constructed and artistically developed of all—'s"—here insert name of author—"many masterly productions. The genius of the author has enabled him skilfully to portray the atmosphere and characters of the period. The scene is laid in and the time roughly is that of the—th century. The hero is—; the heroine,—; and after numerous obstacles and ingenious complications they eventually marry. The character of the old—"—here insert father, mother, uncle or grandparent, gardener or family servant—"is delightfully whimsical and humorous, and full of subtle touches. The tragic element is furnished by—, the—. The author touches with keen satire on the follies and vices of the time, while the interest in the principal love affair is sustained until the final dénouement. Altogether it would be difficult to imagine a more brilliant example of dramatic—or literary—art."

I give this rather shocking example of sophomoric shiftlessness for the purpose of illustrating my attitude toward my educational opportunities and what was possible in the way of dexterously avoiding them. All I had to do was to learn the names of the chief characters in the various plays and novels prescribed. If I could acquire a brief scenario of each so much the better. Invariably they had heroes and heroines, good old servants or grandparents, and merry jesters. At the examination I successfully simulated familiarity with a book I had never read and received a commendatory mark.

This happy-go-lucky frame of mind was by no means peculiar to myself. Indeed I believe it to have been shared by the great majority of my classmates. The result was that we were sent forth into the world without having mastered any subject whatsoever, or even followed it for a sufficient length of time to become sincerely interested in it. The only study I pursued more than one year was English composition, which came easily to me, and which in one form or another I followed throughout my course. Had I adopted the same tactics with any other of the various branches open to me, such as history, chemistry or languages, I should not be what I am to-day—a hopelessly superficial man.

Mind you, I do not mean to assert that I got nothing out of it at all. Undoubtedly I absorbed a smattering of a variety of subjects that might on a pinch pass for education. I observed how men with greater social advantages than myself brushed their hair, wore their clothes and took off their hats to their women friends. Frankly that was about everything I took away with me. I was a victim of that liberality of opportunity which may be a heavenly gift to a post-graduate in a university, but which is intellectual damnation to an undergraduate collegian.

The chief fault that I have to find with my own education, however, is that at no time was I encouraged to think for myself. No older man ever invited me to his study, there quietly and frankly to discuss the problems of human existence. I was left entirely vague as to what it was all about, and the relative values of things were never indicated. The same emphasis was placed on everything—whether it happened to be the Darwinian Theory, the Fall of Jerusalem or the character of Ophelia.

I had no philosophy, no theory of morals, and no one ever even attempted to explain to me what religion or the religious instinct was supposed to be. I was like a child trying to build a house and gathering materials of any substance, shape or color without regard to the character of the intended edifice. I was like a man trying to get somewhere and taking whatever paths suited his fancy—first one and then another, irrespective of where they led. The Why and the Wherefore were unknown questions to me, and I left the university without any idea as to how I came to be in the world or what my duties toward my fellowmen might be.

In a word the two chief factors in education passed me by entirely—(a) my mind received no discipline; (b) and the fundamental propositions of natural philosophy were neither brought to my attention nor explained to me. These deficiencies have never been made up. Indeed, as to the first, my mind, instead of being developed by my going to college, was seriously injured. My memory has never been good since and my methods of reading and thinking are hurried and slipshod, but this is a small thing compared with the lack of any philosophy of life. I acquired none as a youth and I have never had any since. For fifty years I have existed without any guiding purpose except blindly to get ahead—without any religion, either natural or dogmatic. I am one of a type—a pretty good, perfectly aimless man, without any principles at all.

They tell me that things have changed at the universities since my day and that the elective system is no longer in favor. Judging by my own case, the sooner it is abolished entirely, the better for the undergraduate. I should, however, suggest one important qualification—namely, that a boy be given the choice in his Freshman year of three or four general subjects, such as philosophy, art, history, music, science, languages or literature, and that he should be compelled to follow the subjects he elects throughout his course.

In addition I believe the relation of every study to the whole realm of knowledge should be carefully explained. Art cannot be taught apart from history; history cannot be grasped independently of literature. Religion, ethics, science and philosophy are inextricably involved one with another.

But mere learning or culture, a knowledge of facts or of arts, is unimportant as compared with a realization of the significance of life. The one is superficial—the other is fundamental; the one is temporal—the other is spiritual. There is no more wretched human being than a highly trained but utterly purposeless man—which, after all, is only saying that there is no use in having an education without a religion; that unless someone is going to live in the house there is not much use in elaborately furnishing it.

I am not attempting to write a treatise on pedagogy; but, when all is said, I am inclined to the belief that my unfortunate present condition, whatever my material success may have been, is due to lack of education—in philosophy in its broadest sense; in mental discipline; and in actual acquirement.

It is in this last field that my deficiencies and those of my class are superficially most apparent. A wide fund of information may be less important than a knowledge of general principles, but it is none the less valuable; and all of us ought to be equipped with the kind of education that will enable us to understand the world of men as well as the world of nature.

It is, of course, essential for us to realize that the physical characteristics of a continent may have more influence on the history of nations than mere wars or battles, however far-reaching the foreign policies of their rulers; but, in addition to an appreciation of this and similar underlying propositions governing the development of civilization, the educated man who desires to study the problems of his own time and country, to follow the progress of science and philosophy, and to enjoy music, literature and art, must have a certain elementary equipment of mere facts.

The Oriental attitude of mind that enabled the Shah of Persia calmly to decline the invitation of the Prince of Wales to attend the Derby, on the ground that "he knew one horse could run faster than another," is foreign to that of Western civilization. The Battle of Waterloo is a flyspeck in importance contrasted with the problem of future existence; but the man who never heard of Napoleon would make a dull companion in this world or the next.

We live in direct proportion to the keenness of our interest in life; and the wider and broader this interest is, the richer and happier we are. A man is as big as his sympathies, as small as his selfishness. The yokel thinks only of his dinner and his snooze under the hedge, but the man of education rejoices in every new production of the human brain.

Advantageous intercourse between civilized human beings requires a working knowledge of the elementary facts of history, of the achievements in art, music and letters, as well as of the principles of science and philosophy. When people go to quarreling over the importance of a particular phase of knowledge or education they are apt to forget that, after all, it is a purely relative matter, and that no one can reasonably belittle the value of any sort of information. But furious arguments arise over the question as to how history should be taught, and "whether a boy's head should be crammed full of dates." Nobody in his senses would want a boy's head crammed full of dates any more than he would wish his stomach stuffed with bananas; but both the head and the stomach need some nourishment—better dates than nothing.

If a knowledge of a certain historical event is of any value whatsoever, the greater and more detailed our knowledge the better—including perhaps, but not necessarily, its date. The question is not essentially whether the dates are of value, but how much emphasis should be placed on them to the exclusion of other facts of history.

"There is no use trying to remember dates," is a familiar cry. There is about as much sense in such a statement as the announcement: "There is no use trying to remember who wrote Henry Esmond, composed the Fifth Symphony, or painted the Last Supper." There is a lot of use in trying to remember anything. The people who argue to the contrary are too lazy to try.

* * * * *

I suppose it may be conceded, for the sake of argument, that every American, educated or not, should know the date of the Declaration of Independence, and have some sort of acquaintance with the character and deeds of Washington. If we add to this the date of the discovery of America and the first English settlement; the inauguration of the first president; the Louisiana Purchase; the Naval War with England; the War with Mexico; the Missouri Compromise, and the firing on Fort Sumter, we cannot be accused of pedantry. It certainly could not do any one of us harm to know these dates or a little about the events themselves.

This is equally true, only in a lesser degree, in regard to the history of foreign nations. Any accurate knowledge is worth while. It is harder, in the long run, to remember a date slightly wrong than with accuracy. The dateless man, who is as vague as I am about the League of Cambray or Philip II, will loudly assert that the trouble incident to remembering a date in history is a pure waste of time. He will allege that "a general idea"—a very favorite phrase—is all that is necessary. In the case of such a person you can safely gamble that his so-called "general idea" is no idea at all. Pin him down and he will not be able to tell you within five hundred years the dates of some of the cardinal events of European history—the invasion of

Europe by the Huns, for instance. Was it before or after Christ? He might just as well try to tell you that it was quite enough to know that our Civil War occurred somewhere in the nineteenth century.

I have personally no hesitation in advancing the claim that there are a few elementary principles and fundamental facts in all departments of human knowledge which every person who expects to derive any advantage from intelligent society should not only once learn but should forever remember. Not to know them is practically the same thing as being without ordinary means of communication. One may not find it necessary to remember the binomial theorem or the algebraic formula for the contents of a circle, but he should at least have a formal acquaintance with Julius Caesar, Hannibal, Charlemagne, Martin Luther, Francis I, Queen Elizabeth, Louis XIV, Napoleon I—and a dozen or so others. An educated man must speak the language of educated men.

I do not think it too much to demand that in history he should have in mind, at least approximately, one important date in each century in the chronicles of France, England, Italy and Germany. That is not much, but it is a good start. And shall we say ten dates in American history? He should, in addition, have a rough working knowledge of the chief personages who lived in these centuries and were famous in war, diplomacy, art, religion and literature. His one little date will at least give him some notion of the relation the events in one country bore to those in another.

I boldly assert that in a half hour you can learn by heart all the essential dates in American history. I assume that you once knew, and perhaps still know, something about the events themselves with which they are connected. Ten minutes a day for the rest of the week and you will have them at your fingers' ends. It is no trick at all. It is as easy as learning the names of the more important parts of the mechanism of your motor. There is nothing impossible or difficult, or even tedious, about it; but it seems Herculean because you have never taken the trouble to try to remember anything. It is the same attitude that renders it almost physically painful for one of us to read over the scenario of an opera or a column biography of its composer before hearing a performance at the Metropolitan. Yet fifteen minutes or half an hour invested in this way pays about five hundred per cent.

And the main thing, after you have learned anything, is not to forget it. Knowledge forgotten is no knowledge at all. That is the trouble with the elective system as usually administered in our universities. At the end of the college year the student tosses aside his Elements of Geology and forgets everything between its covers. What he has learned should be made the basis for other and more

79

detailed knowledge. The instructor should go on building a superstructure on the foundation he has laid, and at the end of his course the aspirant for a diploma should be required to pass an examination on his entire college work. Had I been compelled to do that, I should probably be able to tell now—what I do not know— whether Melancthon was a painter, a warrior, a diplomat, a theologian or a dramatic poet.

I have instanced the study of dates because they are apt to be the storm center of discussions concerning education. It is fashionable to scoff at them in a superior manner. We all of us loathe them; yet they are as indispensable—a certain number of them—as the bones of a body. They make up the skeleton of history. They are the orderly pegs on which we can hang later acquired information. If the pegs are not there the information will fall to the ground.

For example, our entire conception of the Reformation, or of any intellectual or religious movement, might easily turn on whether it preceded or followed the discovery of printing; and our mental picture of any great battle, as well as our opinion of the strategy of the opposing armies, would depend on whether or not gunpowder had been invented at the time. Hence the importance of a knowledge of the dates of the invention of printing and of gunpowder in Europe.

It is ridiculous to allege that there is no minimum of education, to say nothing of culture, which should be required of every intelligent human being if he is to be but a journeyman in society. In an unconvincing defense of our own ignorance we loudly insist that detailed knowledge of any subject is mere pedagogy, a hindrance to clear thinking, a superfluity. We do not say so, to be sure, with respect to knowledge in general; but that is our attitude in regard to any particular subject that may be brought up. Yet to deny the value of special information is tantamount to an assertion of the desirability of general ignorance. It is only the politician who can afford to say: "Wide knowledge is a fatal handicap to forcible expression."

This is not true of the older countries. In Germany, for instance, a knowledge of natural philosophy, languages and history is insisted on. To the German schoolboy, George Washington is almost as familiar a character as Columbus; but how many American children know anything of Bismarck? The ordinary educated foreigner speaks at least two languages and usually three, is fairly well grounded in science, and is perfectly familiar with ancient and modern history. The American college graduate seems like a child beside him so far as these things are concerned.

We are content to live a hand-to-mouth mental existence on a haphazard diet of newspapers and the lightest novels. We are too lazy to take the trouble either to discipline our minds or to acquire, as adults, the elementary knowledge necessary to enable us to read intelligently even rather superficial books on important questions vitally affecting our own social, physical intellectual or moral existences.

If somebody refers to Huss or Wyclif ten to one we do not know of whom he is talking; the same thing is apt to be true about the draft of the hot-water furnace or the ball and cock of the tank in the bathroom. Inertia and ignorance are the handmaidens of futility. Heaven forbid that we should let anybody discover this aridity of our minds!

My wife admits privately that she has forgotten all the French she ever knew—could not even order a meal from a carte de jour; yet she is a never-failing source of revenue to the counts and marquises who yearly rush over to New York to replenish their bank accounts by giving parlor lectures in their native tongue on Le XIIIme Siècle or Madame Lebrun. No one would ever guess that she understands no more than one word out of twenty and that she has no idea whether Talleyrand lived in the fifteenth or the eighteenth century, or whether Calvin was a Frenchman or a Scotchman.

Our clever people are content merely with being clever. They will talk Tolstoi or Turgenieff with you, but they are quite vague about Catherine II or Peter the Great. They are up on D'Annunczio, but not on Garibaldi or Cavour. Our ladies wear a false front of culture, but they are quite bald underneath.

* * * * *

Being educated, however, does not consist, by any means, in knowing who fought and won certain battles or who wrote the Novum Organum. It lies rather in a knowledge of life based on the experience of mankind. Hence our study of history. But a study of history in the abstract is valueless. It must be concrete, real and living to have any significance for us. The schoolboy who learns by rote imagines the Greeks as outline figures of one dimension, clad in helmets and tunics, and brandishing little swords. That is like thinking of Jeanne d'Arc as a suit of armor or of Theodore Roosevelt as a pair of spectacles.

If the boy is to gain anything by his acquaintance with the Greeks he must know what they ate and drank, how they amused themselves, what they talked about, and what they believed as to the nature and origin of the universe and the probability of a future life. I hold that it is as important to know how the Romans told time as that Nero fiddled while his capital was burning. William the Silent was once just as much alive as P.T. Barnum, and a great deal more worth while. It is fatal to regard historical personages as lay figures and not as human beings.

We are equally vague with respect to the ordinary processes of our daily lives. I have not the remotest idea of how to make a cup of coffee or disconnect the gas or water mains in my own house. If my sliding door sticks I send for the carpenter, and if water trickles in the tank I telephone for the plumber. I am a helpless infant in the stable and my motor is the creation of a Frankenstein that has me at its mercy. My wife may recall something of cookery—which she would not admit, of course, before the butler—but my daughters have never been inside a kitchen. None of my family knows anything about housekeeping or the prices of foodstuffs or house-furnishings. My coal and wood are delivered and paid for without my inquiring as to the correctness of the bills, and I offer the same temptations to dishonest tradesmen that a drunken man does to pickpockets. Yet I complain of the high cost of living!

My family has never had the slightest training in practical affairs. If we were cast away on a fertile tropical island we should be forced to subsist on bananas and clams, and clothe ourselves with leaves,—provided the foliage was ready made and came in regulation sizes.

These things are vastly more important from an educational point of view than a knowledge of the relationship of Mary Stuart to the Duke of Guise, however interesting that may be to a reader of French history of the sixteenth century. A knowledge of the composition of gunpowder is more valuable than of Guy Fawkes' Gunpowder Plot. If we know nothing about household economies we can hardly be expected to take an interest in the problems of the proletariat. If we are ignorant of the fundamental data of sociology and politics we can have no real opinions on questions affecting the welfare of the people.

The classic phrase "The public be damned!" expresses our true feeling about the matter. We cannot become excited about the wrongs and hardships of the working class when we do not know and do not care how they live. One of my daughters—aged seven— once essayed a short story, of which the heroine was an orphan child in direst want. It began: "Corrine was starving. 'Alas! What shall we do for food?' she asked her French nurse as they entered the carriage for their afternoon drive in the park." I have no doubt that even to-day this same young lady supposes that there are porcelain baths in every tenement house.

I myself have no explanation as to why I pay eighty dollars for a business suit any my bookkeepers seems to be equally well turned out for eighteen dollars and fifty cents. That is essentially why the people have an honest and well-founded distrust of those enthusiastic society ladies who rush into charity and frantically engage in the elevation of the masses. The poor working girl is apt to know a good deal more about her own affairs than the Fifth Avenue matron with an annual income of three hundred and fifty thousand dollars.

If I were doing it all over again—and how I wish I could!—I should insist on my girls being taught not only music and languages but cooking, sewing, household economy and stenography. They should at least be able to clothe and feed themselves and their children if somebody supplied them with the materials, and to earn a living if the time came when they had to do it. They have now no conception of the relative values of even material things, what the things are made of or how they are put together. For them hats, shoes, French novels and roast chicken can be picked off the trees.

* * * * *

This utter ignorance of actual life not only keeps us at a distance from the people of our own time but renders our ideas of history equally vague, abstract and unprofitable. I believe it would be an excellent thing if, beginning with the age of about ten years, no child were allowed to eat anything until he was able to tell where it was produced, what it cost and how it was prepared. If this were carried out in every department of the child's existence he would have small need of the superficial education furnished by most of our institutions of learning. Our children are taught about the famines of history when they cannot recognize a blade of wheat or tell the price of a loaf of bread, or how it is made.

I would begin the education of my boy—him of the tango and balkline billiards—with a study of himself, in the broad use of the term, before I allowed him to study about other people or the history of nations. I would seat him in a chair by the fire and begin with his feet. I would inquire what he knew about his shoes—what they were made of, where the substance came from, the cost of its production, the duty on leather, the process of manufacture, the method of transportation of goods, freight rates, retailing, wages, repairs, how shoes were polished—this would begin, if desired, a new line of inquiry as to the composition of said polish, cost, and so on—comparative durability of hand and machine work, introduction of machines into England and its effect on industrial conditions. I say I would do all this; but, of course, I could not. I would have to be an educated man in the first place. Why, beginning with that dusty little pair of shoes, my boy and I might soon be deep in Interstate Commerce and the Theory of Malthus—on familiar terms with Thomas A. Edison and Henry George!

And the next time my son read about a Tammany politician giving away a pair of shoes to each of his adherents it would mean something to him—as much as any other master stroke of diplomacy.

I would instruct every boy in a practical knowledge of the house in which he lives, give him a familiarity with simple tools and a knowledge of how to make small repairs and to tinker with the water pipes. I would teach him all those things I now do not know myself—where the homeless man can find a night's lodging; how to get a disorderly person arrested; why bottled milk costs fifteen cents a quart; how one gets his name on the ballot if he wants to run for alderman; where the Health Department is located, and how to get vaccinated for nothing.

By the time we had finished we would be in a position to understand the various editorials in the morning papers which now we do not read. Far more than that, my son would be brought to a realization that everything in the world is full of interest for the man who has the knowledge to appreciate its significance. "A primrose by a river's brim" should be no more suggestive, even to a lake-poet, than a Persian rug or a rubber shoe. Instead of the rug he will have a vision of the patient Afghan in his mountain village working for years with unrequited industry; instead of the shoe he will see King Leopold and hear the lamentations of the Congo.

My ignorance of everything beyond my own private bank account and stomach is due to the fact that I have selfishly and foolishly regarded these two departments as the most important features of my existence. I now find that my financial and gastronomical satisfaction has been purchased at the cost of an infinite delight in other things. I am mentally out of condition.

Apart from this brake on the wheel of my intelligence, however, I suffer an even greater impediment by reason of the fact that, never having acquired a thorough groundwork of elementary knowledge, I find I cannot read with either pleasure or profit. Most adult essays or histories presuppose some such foundation.

Recently I have begun to buy primers—such as are used in the elementary schools—in order to acquire the information that should have been mine at twenty years of age. And I have resolved that in my daily reading of the newspapers I will endeavor to look up on the map and remember the various places concerning which I read any news item of importance, and to assimilate the facts themselves. It is my intention also to study, at least half an hour each day, some simple treatise on science, politics, art, letters or history. In this way I hope to regain some of my interest in the activities of mankind. If I cannot do this I realize now that it will go hard with me in the years that are drawing nigh. I shall, indeed, then lament that "I have no pleasure in them."

* * * * *

It is the common practice of business men to say that when they reach a certain age they are going to quit work and enjoy themselves. How this enjoyment is proposed to be attained varies in the individual case. One man intends to travel or live abroad—usually, he believes, in Paris. Another is going into ranching or farming. Still another expects to give himself up to art, music and books. We all have visions of the time when we shall no longer have to go downtown every day and can indulge in those pleasures that are now beyond our reach.

Unfortunately the experience of humanity demonstrates the inevitability of the law of Nature which prescribes that after a certain age it is practically impossible to change our habits, either of work or of play, without physical and mental misery.

Most of us take some form of exercise throughout our lives—riding, tennis, golf or walking. This we can continue to enjoy in moderation after our more strenuous days are over; but the manufacturer, stock broker or lawyer who thinks that after his sixtieth birthday he is going to be able to find permanent happiness on a farm, loafing round Paris or reading in his library will be sadly disappointed. His habit of work will drive him back, after a year or so of wretchedness, to the factory, the ticker or the law office; and his habit of play will send him as usual to the races, the club or the variety show.

One cannot acquire an interest by mere volition. It is a matter of training and of years. The pleasures of to-day will eventually prove to be the pleasures of our old age—provided they continue to be pleasures at all, which is more than doubtful.

As we lose the capacity for hard work we shall find that we need something to take its place—something more substantial and less unsatisfactory than sitting in the club window or taking in the

85

Broadway shows. But, at least, the seeds of these interests must be sown now if we expect to gather a harvest this side of the grave.

What is more natural than to believe that in our declining years we shall avail ourselves of the world's choicest literature and pass at least a substantial portion of our days in the delightful companionship of the wisest and wittiest of mankind? That would seem to be one of the happiest uses to which good books could be put; but the hope is vain. The fellow who does not read at fifty will take no pleasure in books at seventy.

My club is full of dozens of melancholy examples of men who have forgotten how to read. They have spent their entire lives perfecting the purely mechanical aspects of their existences. The mind has practically ceased to exist, so far as they are concerned. They have built marvelous mansions, where every comfort is instantly furnished by contrivances as complicated and accurate as the machinery of a modern warship. The doors and windows open and close, the lights are turned on and off, and the elevator stops—all automatically. If the temperature of a room rises above a certain degree the heating apparatus shuts itself off; if it drops too low something else happens to put it right again. The servants are swift, silent and decorous. The food is perfection. Their motors glide noiselessly to and fro. Their establishments run like fine watches.

They have had to make money to achieve this mechanical perfection; they have had no time for anything else during their active years. And, now that those years are over, they have nothing to do. Their minds are almost as undeveloped as those of professional pugilists. Dinners and drinks, backgammon and billiards, the lightest opera, the trashiest novels, the most sensational melodrama are the most elevating of their leisure's activities. Read? Hunt? Farm? Not much! They sit behind the plate-glass windows and bet on whether more limousines will go north than south in the next ten minutes.

If you should ask one of them whether he had read some book that was exciting discussion among educated people at the moment, he would probably look at you blankly and, after remarking that he had never cared for economics or history—as the case might be—inquire whether you preferred a "Blossom" or a "Tornado." Poor vacuous old cocks! They might be having a green and hearty old age, surrounded by a group of the choicest spirits of all time.

Upstairs in the library there are easy-chairs within arm's reach of the best fellows who ever lived—adventurers, story-tellers, novelists, explorers, historians, rhymers, fighters, essayists, vagabonds and general liars—Immortals, all of them.

You can take your pick and if he bores you send him packing without a word of apology. They are good friends to grow old with—friends who in hours of weariness, of depression or of gladness may be summoned at will by those of us who belong to the Brotherhood of Educated Men—of which, alas! I and my associates are no longer members.

CHAPTER V

MY MORALS

The concrete evidence of my success as represented by my accumulated capital—outside of my uptown dwelling house—amounts, as I have previously said, to about seven hundred and fifty thousand dollars. This is invested principally in railroad and mining stocks, both of which are subject to considerable fluctuation; and I have also substantial holdings in industrial corporations. Some of these companies I represent professionally. As a whole, however, my investments may be regarded as fairly conservative. At any rate they cause me little uneasiness.

My professional income is regular and comes with surprisingly little effort. I have as clients six manufacturing corporations that pay me retainers of twenty-five hundred dollars each, besides my regular fees for services rendered. I also represent two banks and a trust company.

All this is fixed business and most of it is attended to by younger men, whom I employ at moderate salaries. I do almost no detail work myself, and my junior partners relieve me of the drawing of even important papers; so that, though I am constantly at my office, my time is spent in advising and consulting.

I dictate all my letters and rarely take a pen in my hand. Writing has become laborious and irksome. I even sign my correspondence with an ingenious rubber stamp that imitates my scrawling signature beyond discovery. If I wish to know the law on some given point I press a button and tell my managing clerk what I want. In an hour or two he hands me the authorities covering the issue in question in typewritten form. It is extraordinarily simple and easy. Yet only yesterday I heard of a middle-aged man, whom I knew to be a peculiarly well-equipped all-around lawyer, who was ready to give up his private practice and take a place in any reputable office at a salary of thirty-five hundred dollars!

Most of my own time is spent in untangling mixed puzzles of law and fact, and my clients are comparatively few in number, though their interests are large. Thus I see the same faces over and over again. I lunch daily at a most respectable eating club; and here, too, I meet the same men over and over again. I rarely make a new acquaintance downtown; in fact I rarely leave my office during the day. If I need to confer with any other attorney I telephone. There are dozens of lawyers in New York whose voices I know well—yet whose faces I have never seen.

My office is on the nineteenth floor of a white marble building, and I can look down the harbor to the south and up the Hudson to the north. I sit there in my window like a cliffdweller at the mouth of his cave. When I walk along Wall Street I can look up at many other hundreds of these caves, each with its human occupant. We leave our houses uptown, clamber down into a tunnel called the Subway, are shot five miles or so through the earth, and debouch into an elevator that rushes us up to our caves. Only between my house and the entrance to the Subway am I obliged to step into the open air at all. A curious life! And I sit in my chair and talk to people in multitudes of other caves near by, or caves in New Jersey, Washington or Chicago.

Louis XI used to be called "the human spider" by reason of his industry, but we modern office men are far more like human spiders than he, as we sit in the center of our webs of invisible wires. We wait and wait, and our lines run out across the length and breadth of the land—sometimes getting tangled, to be sure, so that it is frequently difficult to decide just which spider owns the web; but we sit patiently doing nothing save devising the throwing out of other lines.

We weave, but we do not build; we manipulate, buy, sell and lend, quarrel over the proceeds, and cover the world with our nets, while the ants and the bees of mankind labor, construct and manufacture, and struggle to harness the forces of Nature. We plan and others execute. We dicker, arrange, consult, cajole, bribe, pull our wires and extort; but we do it all in one place—the center of our webs and the webs are woven in our caves.

I figure that I spend about six hours each day in my office; that I sleep nearly nine hours; that I am in transit on surface cars and in subways at least one hour and a half more; that I occupy another hour and a half in bathing, shaving and dressing, and an hour lunching at midday. This leaves a margin of five hours a day for all other activities.

Could even a small portion of this time be spent consecutively in reading in the evening, I could keep pace with current thought and literature much better than I do; or if I spent it with my son and daughters I should know considerably more about them than I do now, which is practically nothing. But the fact is that every evening from the first of November to the first of May the motor comes to the door at five minutes to eight and my wife and I are whirled up or down town to a dinner party—that is, save on those occasions when eighteen or twenty people are whirled to us.

89

* * * * *

This short recital of my daily activities is sufficient to demonstrate that I lead an exceedingly narrow and limited existence. I do not know any poor men, and even the charities in which I am nominally interested are managed by little groups of rich ones. The truth is, I learned thirty years ago that if one wants to make money one must go where money is and cultivate the people who have it. I have no petty legal business—there is nothing in it. If I cannot have millionaires for clients I do not want any. The old idea that the young country lawyer could shove a pair of socks into his carpetbag, come to the great city, hang out his shingle and build up a practice has long since been completely exploded. The best he can do now is to find a clerkship at twelve hundred dollars a year.

Big business gravitates to the big offices; and when the big firms look round for junior partners they do not choose the struggling though brilliant young attorney from the country, no matter how large his general practice may have become; but they go after the youth whose father is a director in forty corporations or the president of a trust.

In the same way what time I have at my disposal to cultivate new acquaintances I devote not to the merely rich and prosperous but to the multi-millionaire—if I can find him—who does not even know the size of his income. I have no time to waste on the man who is simply earning enough to live quietly and educate his family. He cannot throw anything worth while in my direction; but a single crumb from the magnate's table may net me twenty or thirty thousand dollars. Thus, not only for social but for business reasons, successful men affiliate habitually only with rich people. I concede that is a rather sordid admission, but it is none the truth.

* * * * *

Money is the symbol of success; it is what we are all striving to get, and we naturally select the ways and means best adapted for the purpose. One of the simplest is to get as near it as possible and stay there. If I make a friend of a struggling doctor or professor he may invite me to draw his will, which I shall either have to do for nothing or else charge him fifty dollars for; but the railroad president with whom I often lunch, and who is just as agreeable personally, may perhaps ask me to reorganize a railroad. I submit that, selfish as it all seems when I write it down, it would be hard to do otherwise.

I do not deliberately examine each new candidate for my

90

friendship and select or reject him in accordance with a financial test; but what I do is to lead a social and business life that will constantly throw me only with rich and powerful men. I join only rich men's clubs; I go to resorts in the summer frequented only by rich people; and I play only with those who can, if they will, be of advantage to me. I do not do this deliberately; I do it instinctively— now. I suppose at one time it was deliberate enough, but to-day it comes as natural as using my automobile instead of a street car.

We have heard a great deal recently about a so-called Money Trust. The truth of the matter is that the Money Trust is something vastly greater than any mere aggregation of banks; it consists in our fundamental trust in money. It is based on our instinctive and ineradicable belief that money rules the destinies of mankind.

Everything is estimated by us in money. A man is worth so and so much—in dollars. The millionaire takes precedence of everybody, except at the White House. The rich have things their own way—and every one knows it. Ashamed of it? Not at all. We are the greatest snobs in the civilized world, and frankly so. We worship wealth because at present we desire only the things wealth can buy.

The sea, the sky, the mountains, the clear air of autumn, the simple sports and amusements of our youth and of the comparatively poor, pleasures in books, in birds, in trees and flowers, are disregarded for the fierce joys of acquisition, of the ownership in stocks and bonds, or for the no less keen delight in the display of our own financial superiority over our fellows.

We know that money is the key to the door of society. Without it our sons will not get into the polo-playing set or our daughters figure in the Sunday supplements. We want money to buy ourselves a position and to maintain it after we have bought it.

We want house on the sunny side of the street, with façades of graven marble; we want servants in livery and in buttons—or in powder and breeches if possible; we want French chefs and the best wine and tobacco, twenty people to dinner on an hour's notice, supper parties and a little dance afterward at Sherry's or Delmonico's, a box at the opera and for first nights at the theaters, two men in livery for our motors, yachts and thirty-footers, shooting boxes in South Carolina, salmon water in New Brunswick, and regular vacations, besides, at Hot Springs, Aiken and Palm Beach; we want money to throw away freely and like gentlemen at Canfield's, Bradley's and Monte Carlo; we want clubs, country houses, saddle-horses, fine clothes and gorgeously dressed women; we want leisure and laughter, and a trip or so to Europe every year, our names at the top of the society column, a smile from the grand dame in the tiara and a seat at her dinner table—these are the things we want, and since we cannot have them without money we go after the money first, as the sine qua non.

We want these things for ourselves and we want them for our children. We hope our grandchildren will have them also, though about that we do not care so much. We want ease and security and the relief of not thinking whether we can afford to do things. We want to be lords of creation and to pass creation on to our descendants, exactly as did the nobility of the Ancien Régime.

At the present time money will buy anything, from a place in the vestry of a swell church to a seat in the United States Senate—an election to Congress, a judgeship or a post in the diplomatic service. It will buy the favor of the old families or a decision in the courts. Money is the controlling factor in municipal politics in New York. The moneyed group of Wall Street wants an amenable mayor—a Tammany mayor preferred—so that it can put through its contracts. You always know where to find a regular politician. One always knew where to find Dick Croker. So the Traction people pour the contents of their coffers into the campaign bags.

Until very recently the Supreme Court judges of New York bought their positions by making substantial contributions to the Tammany treasury. The inferior judgeships went considerably cheaper. A man who stood in with the Big Boss might get a bargain. I have done business with politicians all my life and I have never found it necessary to mince my words. If I wanted a favor I always asked exactly what it was going to cost—and I always got the favor.

No one needs to hunt very far for cases where the power of money has influenced the bench in recent times. The rich man can buy his son a place in any corporation or manufacturing company. The young man may go in at the bottom, but he will shoot up to the top in a year or two, with surprising agility, over the heads of a couple of thousand other and better men. The rich man can defy the law and scoff at justice; while the poor man, who cannot pay lawyers for delay, goes to prison. These are the veriest platitudes of demagogy, but they are true—absolutely and undeniably true.

We know all this and we act accordingly, and our children imbibe a like knowledge with their mother's or whatever other properly sterilized milk we give them as a substitute. We, they and everybody else know that if enough money can be accumulated the possessor will be on Easy Street for the rest of his life—not merely the Easy Street of luxury and comfort, but of security, privilege and power; and because we like Easy Street rather than the Narrow Path we devote ourselves to getting there in the quickest possible way.

We take no chances on getting our reward in the next world. We want it here and now, while we are sure of it—on Broadway, at

92

Newport or in Paris. We do not fool ourselves any longer into thinking that by self-sacrifice here we shall win happiness in the hereafter. That is all right for the poor, wretched and disgruntled. Even the clergy are prone to find heaven and hell in this world rather than in the life after death; and the decay of faith leads us to feel that a purse of gold in the hand is better than a crown of the same metal in the by-and-by. We are after happiness, and to most of us money spells it.

The man of wealth is protected on every side from the dangers that beset the poor. He can buy health and immunity from anxiety, and he can install his children in the same impregnable position. The dust of his motor chokes the citizen trudging home from work. He soars through life on a cushioned seat, with shock absorbers to alleviate all the bumps. No wonder we trust in money! We worship the golden calf far more than ever did the Israelites beneath the crags of Sinai. The real Money Trust is the tacit conspiracy by which those who have the money endeavor to hang on to it and keep it among themselves. Neither at the present time do great fortunes tend to dissolve as inevitably as formerly.

Oliver Wendell Holmes somewhere analyzes the rapid disintegration of the substantial fortunes of his day and shows how it is, in fact, but "three generations from shirtsleeves to shirtsleeves." A fortune of two hundred thousand dollars divided among four children, each of whose share is divided among four grandchildren, becomes practically nothing at all—in only two. But could the good doctor have observed the tendencies of to-day he would have commented on a new phenomenon, which almost counteracts the other.

It may be, and probably is, the fact that comparatively small fortunes still tend to disintegrate. This was certainly the rule during the first half of the nineteenth century in New England, when there was no such thing as a distinctly moneyed class, and when the millionaire was a creature only of romance. But when, as to-day, fortunes are so large that it is impossible to spend or even successfully give away the income from them, a new element is introduced that did not exist when Doctor Holmes used to meditate in his study on the Back Bay overlooking the placid Charles.

At the present time big fortunes are apt to gain by mere accretion what they lose by division; and the owner of great wealth has opportunities for investment undreamed of by the ordinary citizen who must be content with interest at four per cent and no unearned increment on his capital. This fact might of itself negative the tendency of which he speaks; but there is a much more potent force working against it as well. That is the absolute necessity,

93

induced by the demands of modern metropolitan life, of keeping a big fortune together—or, if it must be divided, of rehabilitating it by marriage.

There was a time not very long ago when one rarely heard of a young man or young woman of great wealth marrying anybody with an equal fortune. To do so was regarded with disapproval, and still is in some communities. To-day it is the rule instead of the exception. Now we habitually speak in America of the "alliances of great families." There are two reasons for this—first, that being a multi-millionaire is becoming, as it were, a sort of recognized profession, having its own sports, its own methods of business and its own interests; second, that the luxury of to-day is so enervating and insidious that a girl or youth reared in what is called society cannot be comfortable, much less happy, on the income of less than a couple of million dollars.

As seems to be demonstrated by the table of my own modest expenditure in a preceding article, the income of but a million dollars will not support any ordinary New York family in anything like the luxury to which the majority of our young people—even the sons and daughters of men in moderate circumstances—are accustomed.

Our young girls are reared on the choicest varieties of food, served with piquant sauces to tempt their appetites; they are permitted to pick and choose, and to refuse what they think they do not like; they are carried to and from their schools, music and dancing lessons in motors, and are taught to regard public conveyances as unhealthful and inconvenient; they never walk; they are given clothes only a trifle less fantastic and bizarre than those of their mothers, and command the services of maids from their earliest years; they are taken to the theater and the hippodrome, and for the natural pleasures of childhood are given the excitement of the footlights and the arena.

As they grow older they are allowed to attend late dances that necessitate remaining in bed the next morning until eleven or twelve o'clock; they are told that their future happiness depends on their ability to attract the right kind of man; they are instructed in every art save that of being useful members of society; and in the ease, luxury and vacuity with which they are surrounded their lives parallel those of demi-mondaines. Indeed, save for the marriage ceremony, there is small difference between them. The social butterfly flutters to the millionaire as naturally as the night moth of the Tenderloin. Hence the tendency to marry money is greater than ever before in the history of civilization.

Frugal, thrifty lives are entirely out of fashion. The solid, self-respecting class, which wishes to associate with people of equal means, is becoming smaller and smaller. If an ambitious mother cannot afford to rent a cottage at Newport or Bar Harbor she takes her daughter to a hotel or boarding house there, in the hope that she will be thrown in contact with young men of wealth. The young girl in question, whose father is perhaps a hardworking doctor or business man, at home lives simply enough; but sacrifices are made to send her to a fashionable school, where her companions fill her ears with stories of their motors, trips to Europe, and the balls they attend during the vacations. She becomes inoculated with the poison of social ambition before she comes out.

Unable by reason of the paucity of the family resources to buy luxuries for herself, she becomes a parasite and hanger-on of rich girls. If she is attractive and vivacious so much the better. Like the shopgirl blinded by the glare of Broadway, she flutters round the drawing rooms and country houses of the ultra-rich seeking to make a match that will put luxury within her grasp; but her chances are not so good as formerly.

To-day the number of large fortunes has increased so rapidly that the wealthy young man has no difficulty in choosing an equally wealthy mate whose mental and physical attractions appear, and doubtless are, quite as desirable as those of the daughter of poorer parents. The same instinct to which I have confessed myself, as a professional man, is at work among our daughters and sons. They may not actually judge individuals by the sordid test of their ability to purchase ease and luxury, but they take care to meet and associate with only those who can do so.

In this their parents are their ofttimes unconscious accomplices. The worthy young man of chance acquaintance is not invited to call—or, if he is, is not pressed to stay to dinner. "Oh, he does not know our crowd!" explains the girl to herself. The crowd, on analysis, will probably be found to contain only the sons and daughters of fathers and mothers who can entertain lavishly and settle a million or so on their offspring at marriage.

There is a constant attraction of wealth for wealth. Poverty never attracted anything. If our children have money of their own that is a good reason to us why they should marry more money. We snarl angrily at the penniless youth, no matter how capable and intelligent, who dares cast his eyes on our daughter. We make it quite unambiguous that we have other plans for her—plans that usually include a steam yacht and a shooting box north of Inverness.

There is nothing more vicious than the commonly expressed desire of parents in merely moderate circumstances to give their children what are ordinarily spoken of as "opportunities." "We wish

95

our daughters to have every opportunity—the best opportunities," they say, meaning an equal chance with richer girls of qualifying themselves for attracting wealthy men and of placing themselves in their way. In reality opportunities for what?—of being utterly miserable for the rest of their lives unless they marry out of their own class.

The desire to get ahead that is transmitted from the American business man to his daughter is the source of untold bitterness—for, though he himself may fail in his own struggle, he has nevertheless had the interest of the game; but she, an old maid, may linger miserably on, unwilling to share the domestic life of some young man more than her equal in every respect.

There is a subtle freemasonry among those who have to do with money. Young men of family are given sinecures in banks and trust companies, and paid many times the salaries their services are worth. The inconspicuous lad who graduates from college the same year as one who comes from a socially prominent family will slave in a downtown office eight hours a day for a thousand dollars a year, while his classmate is bowing in the ladies at the Fifth Avenue Branch—from ten to three o'clock—at a salary of five thousand dollars. Why? Because he knows people who have money and in one way or another may be useful sometime to the president in a social way.

The remuneration of those of the privileged class who do any work at all is on an entirely different basis from that of those who need it. The poor boy is kept on as a clerk, while the rich one is taken into the firm. The old adage says that "Kissing goes by favor"; and favors, financial and otherwise, are given only to those who can offer something in return. The tendency to concentrate power and wealth extends even to the outer rim of the circle. It is an intangible conspiracy to corner the good things and send the poor away empty. As I see it going on round me, it is a heartless business.

Society is like an immense swarm of black bees settled on a honey-pot. The leaders, who flew there first, are at the top, gorged and distended. Round, beneath and on them crawl thousands of others thirsting to feed on the sweet, liquid gold. The pot is covered with them, layer on layer—buzzing hungrily; eager to get as near as possible to the honey, even if they may not taste it. A drop falls on one and a hundred fly on him and lick it off. The air is alive with those who are circling about waiting for an advantageous chance to wedge in between their comrades. They will, with one accord, sting to death any hapless creature who draws near.

* * * * *

Frankly I should not be enough of a man to say these things if my identity were disclosed, however much they ought to be said. Neither should I make the confessions concerning my own career that are to follow; for, though they may evidence a certain shrewdness on my own part, I do not altogether feel that they are to my credit.

When my wife and I first came to New York our aims and ideals were simple enough. I had letters to the head of a rather well-known firm on Wall Street and soon found myself its managing clerk at one hundred dollars a month. The business transacted in the office was big business—corporation work, the handling of large estates, and so on. During three years I was practically in charge of and responsible for the details of their litigations; the net profit divided by the two actual members of the firm was about one hundred and fifty thousand dollars. The gross was about one hundred and eighty thousand, of which twenty thousand went to defray the regular office expenses—including rent, stenographers and ordinary law clerks—while ten thousand was divided among the three men who actually did most of the work.

The first of these was a highly trained lawyer about forty-five years of age, who could handle anything from a dog-license matter before a police justice to the argument of a rebate case in the United States Supreme Court. He was paid forty-five hundred dollars a year and was glad to get it. He was the active man of the office. The second man received thirty-five hundred dollars, and for that sum furnished all the special knowledge needed in drafting railroad mortgages and intricate legal documents of all sorts. The third was a chap of about thirty who tried the smaller cases and ran the less important corporations.

The two heads of the firm devoted most of their time to mixing with bankers, railroad officials and politicians, and spent comparatively little of it at the office; but they got the business—somehow. I suppose they found it because they went out after it. It was doubtless quite legitimate. Somebody must track down the game before the hunter can do the shooting. At any rate they managed to find plenty of it and furnished the work for the other lawyers to do.

I soon made up my mind that in New York brains were a pretty cheap commodity. I was anxious to get ahead; but there was no opening in the firm and there were others ready to take my place the moment it should become vacant. I was a pretty fair lawyer and

97

had laid by in the bank nearly a thousand dollars; so I went to the head of the firm and made the proposition that I should work at the office each day until one o'clock and be paid half of what I was then getting—that is, fifty dollars a month. In the afternoons an understudy should sit at my desk, while I should be free.

I then suggested that the firm might divide with me the proceeds of any business I should bring in. My offer was accepted; and the same afternoon I went to the office of a young stockbroker I knew and stayed there until three o'clock. The next day I did the same thing, and the day after. I did not buy any stocks, but I made myself agreeable to the group about the ticker and formed the acquaintance of an elderly German, who was in the chewing-gum business and who amused himself playing the market.

It was not long before he invited me to lunch with him and I took every opportunity to impress him with my legal acumen. He had a lawyer of his own already, but I soon saw that the impression I was making would have the effect I desired; and presently, as I had confidently expected, he gave me a small legal matter to attend to. Needless to say it was accomplished with care, celerity and success. He gave me another. For six months I dogged that old German's steps every day from one o'clock in the afternoon until twelve at night. I walked, talked, drank beer and played pinochle with him, sat in his library in the evenings, and took him and his wife to the theater.

At the end of that period he discharged his former attorney and retained me. The business was easily worth thirty-five hundred dollars a year, and within a short time the Chicle Trust bought out his interests and I became a director in it and one of its attorneys.

I had already severed my connection with the firm and had opened an office of my own. Among the directors in the trust with whom I was thrown were a couple of rich young men whose fathers had put them on the board merely for purposes of representation. These I cultivated with the same assiduity as I had used with the German. I spent my entire time gunning for big game. I went after the elephants and let the sparrows go. It was only a month or so before my acquaintance with these two boys—for they were little else—had ripened into friendship. My wife and I were invited to visit at their houses and I was placed in contact with their fathers. From these I soon began to get business. I have kept it—kept it to myself. I have no real partners to steal it away from me.

I am now the same kind of lawyer as the two men who composed the firm for which I slaved at a hundred dollars a month. I find the work for my employees to do. I am now an exploiter of labor. It is hardly necessary for me to detail the steps by which I gradually acquired what is known as a gilt-edged practice; but it was not by virtue of my legal abilities, though they are as good as the average. I got it by putting myself in the eye of rich people in every way open to me. I even joined a fashionable church—it pains me to write this—for the sole purpose of becoming a member of the vestry and thus meeting on an intimate footing the half-dozen millionaire merchants who composed it. One of them gave me his business, made me his trustee and executor; and then I resigned from the vestry.

I always made myself persona grata to those who could help me along, wore the best clothes I could buy, never associated with shabby people, and appeared as much as possible in the company of my financial betters. It was the easier for me to do this because my name was not Irish, German or Hebraic. I had a good appearance, manners and an agreeable gloss of culture and refinement. I was tactful, considerate, and tried to strike a personal note in my intercourse with people who were worth while; in fact I made it a practice—and still do so—to send little mementos to my newer acquaintances—a book or some such trifle—with a line expressing my pleasure at having met them.

I know a considerable number of doctors, as well as lawyers, who have built up lucrative practices by making love to their female clients and patients. That I never did; but I always made it a point to flatter any women I took in to dinner, and I am now the trustee or business adviser for at least half a dozen wealthy widows as a direct consequence.

One reason for my success is, I discovered very early in the game that no woman believes she really needs a lawyer. She consults an attorney not for the purpose of getting his advice, but for sympathy and his approval of some course she has already decided on and perhaps already followed. A lawyer who tells a woman the truth thereby loses a client. He has only to agree with her and compliment her on her astuteness and sagacity to intrench himself forever in her confidence.

A woman will do what she wants to do—every time. She goes to a lawyer to explain why she intends to do it. She wants to have a man about on whom she can put the blame if necessary, and is willing to pay—moderately—for the privilege. She talks to a lawyer when no one else is willing to listen to her, and thoroughly enjoys herself. He is the one man who—unless he is a fool—cannot talk back.

Another fact to which I attribute a good deal of my professional éclat is, that I never let any of my social friends forget that I was a lawyer as well as a good fellow; and I always threw a hearty bluff at being prosperous, even when a thousand or two was needed to cover the overdraft in my bank account. It took me about ten years to land myself firmly among the class to which I aspired, and ten years more to make that place impregnable.

To-day we are regarded as one of the older if not one of the old families in New York. I no longer have to lick anybody's boots, and until I began to pen these memoirs I had really forgotten that I ever had. Things come my way now almost of themselves. All I have to do is to be on hand in my office—cheerful, hospitable, with a good story or so always on tap. My junior force does the law work. Yet I challenge anybody to point out anything dishonorable in those tactics by which I first got my feet on the lower rungs of the ladder of success.

It may perhaps be that I should prefer to write down here the story of how, simply by my assiduity and learning, I acquired such a reputation for a knowledge of the law that I was eagerly sought out by a horde of clamoring clients who forced important litigations on me. Things do not happen that way in New York to-day.

Should a young man be blamed for getting on by the easiest way he can? Life is too complex; the population too big. People have no accurate means of finding out who the really good lawyers or doctors are. If you tell them you are at the head of your profession they are apt to believe you, particularly if you wear a beard and are surrounded by an atmosphere of solemnity. Only a man's intimate circle knows where he is or what he is doing at any particular time.

I remember a friend of mine who was an exceedingly popular member of one of the exclusive Fifth Avenue clubs, and who, after going to Europe for a short vacation, decided to remain abroad for a couple of years. At the end of that time he returned to New York hungry for his old life and almost crazy with delight at seeing his former friends. Entering the club about five o'clock he happened to observe one of them sitting by the window. He approached him enthusiastically, slapped him on the shoulder, extended his hand and cried:

"Hello, old man! It's good to see you again!"

The other man looked at him in a puzzled sort of way without moving.

"Hello, yourself!" he remarked languidly. "It's good to see you, all right—but why make so much damned fuss about it?"

The next sentence interchanged between the two developed the fact that he was totally ignorant that his friend had been away at all. This is by no means a fantastic illustration. It happens every day. That is one of the joys of living in New York. You can get drunk, steal a million or so, or run off with another man's wife—and no one will hear about it until you are ready for something else. In such a community it is not extraordinary that most people are taken at their face value. Life moves at too rapid a pace to allow us to find out much about anybody—even our friends. One asks other people to dinner simply because one has seen them at somebody's else house.

I found it at first very difficult—in fact almost impossible—to spur my wife on to a satisfactory cooperation with my efforts to make the hand of friendship feed the mouth of business. She rather indignantly refused to meet my chewing-gum client or call on his wife. She said she preferred to keep her self-respect and stay in the boarding-house where we had resided since we moved to the city; but I demonstrated to her by much argument that it was worse than snobbish not to be decently polite to one's business friends. It was not their fault if they were vulgar. One might even help them to enlarge their lives. Gradually she came round; and as soon as the old German had given me his business she was the first to suggest moving to an apartment hotel uptown.

For a long time, however, she declined to make any genuine social effort. She knew two or three women from our neighborhood who were living in the city, and she used to go and sit with them in the afternoons and sew and help take care of the children. She said they and their husbands were good enough for her and that she had no aspirations toward society. An evening at the theater—in the balcony—every two weeks or so, and a rubber of whist on Saturday night, with a chafing-dish supper afterward, was all the excitement she needed. That was twenty-five years ago. To-day it is I who would put on the brakes, while she insists on shoveling soft coal into the social furnace.

Her metamorphosis was gradual but complete. I imagine that her first reluctance to essay an acquaintance with society arose out of embarrassment and bashfulness. At any rate she no sooner discovered how small a bluff was necessary for success than she easily outdid me in the ingenuity and finesse of her social strategy. It seemed to be instinctive with her. She was always revising her calling lists and cutting out people who were no longer socially useful; and having got what she could out of a new acquaintance, she would forget her as completely as if she had never made her the confidante of her inmost thoughts about other and less socially desirable people.

It seems a bit cold-blooded—this criticism of one's wife; but I know that, however much of a sycophant I may have been in my younger days, my wife has outdone me since then. Presently we were both in the swim, swept off our feet by the current and carried

101

down the river of success, willy-nilly, toward its mouth—to a safe haven, I wonder, or the deluge of a devouring cataract?

* * * * *

The methods I adopted are those in general use, either consciously or unconsciously, among people striving for success in business, politics or society in New York. It is a struggle for existence, precisely like that which goes on in the animal world. Only those who have strength or cunning survive to achieve success. Might makes right to an extent little dreamed of by most of us. Nobody dares to censure or even mildly criticize one who has influence enough to do him harm. We are interested only in safeguarding or adding to the possessions we have already secured. We are wise enough to "play safe." To antagonize one who might assist in depriving us of some of them is contrary to the laws of Nature.

Our thoughts are for ourselves and our children alone. The devil take everybody else! We are safe, warm and comfortable ourselves; we exist without actual labor; and we desire our offspring to enjoy the same ease and safety. The rest of mankind is nothing to us, except a few people it is worth our while to be kind to—personal servants and employees. We should not hesitate to break all ten of the Commandments rather than that we and our children should lose a few material comforts. Anything, save that we should have really to work for a living!

There are essentially two sorts of work: first—genuine labor, which requires all a man's concentrated physical or mental effort; and second—that work which takes the laborer to his office at ten o'clock and, after an easy-going administrative morning, sets him at liberty at three or four.

The officer of an uptown trust company or bank is apt to belong to the latter class. Or perhaps one is in real estate and does business at the dinner tables of his friends. He makes love and money at the same time. His salary and commissions correspond somewhat to the unearned increment on the freeholds in which he deals. These are minor illustrations, but a majority of the administrative positions in our big corporations carry salaries out of all proportion to the services rendered.

These are the places my friends are all looking for—for themselves or their children. The small stockholder would not vote the president of his company a salary of one hundred thousand dollars a year, or the vice-president fifty thousand dollars; but the rich man who controls the stock is willing to give his brother or his nephew a soft snap. From what I know of corporate enterprise in these United States, God save the minority stockholder! But we and our brothers and sons and nephews must live—on Easy Street. We must be able to give expensive dinners and go to the theater and opera, and take our families to Europe—and we can't do it without money.

We must be able to keep up our end without working too hard, to be safe and warm, well fed and smartly turned out, and able to call in a specialist and a couple of trained nurses if one of the children falls ill; we want thirty-five feet of southerly exposure instead of seventeen, menservants instead of maid-servants, and a new motor every two years.

We do not object to working—that is to say, we pride ourselves on having a job. We like to be moderately busy. We would not have enough to amuse us all day if we did not go to the office in the morning; but what we do is not work! It is occupation perhaps—but there is no labor about it, either of mind or body. It is a sinecure—a "cinch." We could stay at home and most of us would not be missed. It is not the seventy-five-hundred-dollar-a-year vice-president but the eight-hundred-and-fifty-dollar clerk for want of whom the machine would stop if he were sick. Our labor is a kind of masculine light housework.

We probably have private incomes, thanks to our fathers or great uncles—not large enough to enable us to cut much of a dash, to be sure, but sufficient to give us confidence—and the proceeds of our daily toil, such as it is, go toward the purchase of luxuries merely. Because we are in business we are able to give bigger and more elegant dinner parties, go to Palm Beach in February, and keep saddle-horses; but we should be perfectly secure without working at all.

Hence we have a sense of independence about it. We feel as if it were rather a favor on our part to be willing to go into an office; and we expect to be paid vastly more proportionately than the fellow who needs the place in order to live: so we cut him out of it at a salary three times what he would have been paid had he got the job, while he keeps on grinding at the books as a subordinate. We come down late and go home early, drop in at the club and go out to dinner, take in the opera, wear furs, ride in automobiles, and generally boss the show—for the sole reason that we belong to the crowd who have the money. Very likely if we had not been born with it we should die from malnutrition, or go to Ward's Island suffering from some variety of melancholia brought on by worry over our inability to make a living.

I read the other day the true story of a little East Side tailor who could not earn enough to support himself and his wife. He became half-crazed from lack of food and together they resolved to commit suicide. Somehow he secured a small 22-caliber rook rifle and a couple of cartridges. The wife knelt down on the bed in her nightgown, with her face to the wall, and repeated a prayer while he shot her in the back. When he saw her sink to the floor dead he became so unnerved that, instead of turning the rifle on himself, he ran out into the street, with chattering teeth, calling for help.

This tragedy was absolutely the result of economic conditions, for the man was a hardworking and intelligent fellow, who could not find employment and who went off his head from lack of nourishment.

Now "I put it to you," as they say in the English law courts, how much of a personal sacrifice would you have made to prevent this tragedy? What would that little East Side Jewess' life have been worth to you? She is dead. Her soul may or may not be with God. As a suicide the Church would say it must be in hell. Well, how much would you have done to preserve her life or keep her soul out of hell?

Frankly, would you have parted with five hundred dollars to save that woman's life? Five hundred dollars? Let me tell you that you would not voluntarily have given up smoking cigars for one year to avoid that tragedy! Of course you would have if challenged to do so. If the fact that the killing could be avoided in some such way or at a certain price, and the discrepancy between the cost and the value of the life were squarely brought to your particular attention, you might and probably would do something. How much is problematical.

Let us do you the credit of saying that you would give five hundred dollars—and take it out of some other charity. But what if you were given another chance to save a life for five hundred dollars? All right; you will save that too. Now a third! You hesitate. That will be spending fifteen hundred dollars—a good deal. Still you decide to do it. Yet how embarrassing! You find an opportunity to save a fourth, a fifth—a hundred lives at the same price! What are you going to do?

We all of us have such a chance in one way or another. The answer is that, in spite of the admonition of Christ to sell our all and give to the poor, and others of His teachings as contained in the Sermon on the Mount, you probably, in order to save the lives of persons unknown to you, would not sacrifice a single substantial material comfort for one year; and that your impulse to save the lives of persons actually brought to your knowledge would diminish,

104

fade away and die in direct proportion to the necessity involved of changing your present luxurious mode of life.

Do you know any rich woman who would sacrifice her automobile in order to send convalescents to the country? She may be a very charitable person and in the habit of sending such people to places where they are likely to recover health; but, no matter how many she actually sends, there would always be eight or ten more who could share in that blessed privilege if she gave up her motor and used the money for the purpose. Yet she does not do so and you do not do so; and, to be quite honest, you would think her a fool if she did.

What an interesting thing it would be if we could see the mental processes of some one of our friends who, unaware of our knowledge of his thoughts, was confronted with the opportunity of saving a life or accomplishing a vast good at a great sacrifice of his worldly possessions!

Suppose, for instance, he could save his own child by spending fifty thousand dollars in doctors, hospitals and nurses. Of course he would do so without a moment's hesitation, even if that was his entire fortune. But suppose the child were a nephew? We see him waver a little. A cousin—there is a distinct pause. Shall he pauperize himself just for a cousin? How about a mere social acquaintance? Not much! He might in a moment of excitement jump overboard to save somebody from drowning; but it would have to be a dear friend or close relative to induce him to go to the bank and draw out all the money he had in the world to save that same life.

The cities are full of lives that can be saved simply by spending a little money; but we close our eyes and, with our pocket-books clasped tight in our hands, pass by on the other side. Why? Not because we do not wish to deprive ourselves of the necessaries of life or even of its solid comforts, but because we are not willing to surrender our amusements. We want to play and not to work. That is what we are doing, what we intend to keep on doing, and what we plan to have our children do after us.

Brotherly love? How can there be such a thing when there is a single sick baby dying for lack of nutrition—a single convalescent suffocating for want of country air—a single family without fire or blankets? Suggest to your wife that she give up a dinner gown and use the money to send a tubercular office boy to the Adirondacks—and listen to her excuses! Is there not some charitable organization that does such things? Has not his family the money? How do you know he really has consumption? Is he a good boy? And finally: "Well, one can't send every sick boy to the country; if one did there would be no money left to bring up one's own children." She hesitates—and the boy dies perhaps! So long as we do not see them dying, we do not really care how many people die.

Our altruism, such as it is, has nothing abstract about it. The successful man does not bother himself about things he cannot see. Do not talk about foreign missions to him. Try his less successful brother—the man who is not successful because you can talk over with him foreign missions or even more idealistic matters; who is a failure because he will make sacrifices for a principle.

It is all a part of our materialism. Real sympathy costs too much money; so we try not to see the miserable creatures who might be restored to health for a couple of hundred dollars. A couple of hundred dollars? Why, you could take your wife to the theater forty times—once a week during the entire season—for that sum!

Poor people make sacrifices; rich ones do not. There is very little real charity among successful people. A man who wasted his time helping others would never get on himself.

* * * * *

It will, of course, be said in reply that the world is full of charitable institutions supported entirely by the prosperous and successful. That is quite true; but it must be remembered that they are small proof in themselves of the amount of real self-sacrifice and genuine charity existing among us.

Philanthropy is largely the occupation of otherwise ineffective people, or persons who have nothing else to do, or of retired capitalists who like the notoriety and laudation they can get in no other way. But, even with philanthropy to amuse him, an idle multi-millionaire in these United States has a pretty hard time of it. He is generally too old to enjoy society and is not qualified to make himself a particularly agreeable companion, even if his manners would pass muster at Newport. Politics is too strenuous. Desirable diplomatic posts are few and the choicer ones still require some dignity or educational qualification in the holders. There is almost nothing left but to haunt the picture sales or buy a city block and order the construction of a French château in the middle of it.

I know one of these men intimately; in fact I am his attorney and helped him make a part of his money. At sixty-four he retired— that is, he ceased endeavoring to increase his fortune by putting up the price of foodstuffs and other commodities, or by driving competitors out of business. Since then he has been utterly wretched. He would like to be in society and dispense a lavish hospitality, but he cannot speak the language of the drawing room. His opera box stands stark and empty. His house, filled with priceless treasures fit for the Metropolitan Museum, is closed nine months in the year.

His own wants are few. His wife is a plain woman, who used to do her own cooking and, in her heart, would like to do it still. He knows nothing of the esthetic side of life and is too old to learn. Once a month, in the season, we dine at his house, with a mixed company, in a desert of dining room at a vast table loaded with masses of gold plate. The peaches are from South Africa; the strawberries from the Riviera. His chef ransacks the markets for pheasants, snipe, woodcock, Egyptian quail and canvasbacks. And at enormous distances from each other—so that the table may be decently full—sit, with their wives, his family doctor, his clergyman, his broker, his secretary, his lawyer, and a few of the more presentable relatives—a merry party! And that is what he has striven, fought and lied for for fifty years.

Often he has told me of the early days, when he worked from seven until six, and then studied in night school until eleven; and of the later ones when he and his wife lived, like ourselves, in a Fourteenth Street lodging house and saved up to go to the theater once a month. As a young man he swore he would have a million before he died. Sunday afternoons he would go up to the Vanderbilt house on Fifth Avenue and, shaking his fist before the ornamental iron railing, whisper savagely that he would own just such a house himself some day. When he got his million he was going to retire. But he got his million at the age of forty-five, and it looked too small and mean; he would have ten—then he would stop!

By fifty-five he had his ten millions. It was comparatively easy, I believe, for him to get it. But still he was not satisfied. Now he has twenty. But apart from his millions, his house and his pictures, which are bought for him by an agent on a salary of ten thousand dollars a year, he has nothing! I dine with him out of charity.

Well, recently Johnson has gone into charity himself. I am told he has given away two millions! That is an exact tenth of his fortune. He is a religious man—in this respect he has outdone most of his brother millionaires. However, he still has an income of over a million a year—enough to satisfy most of his modest needs. Yet the frugality of a lifetime is hard to overcome, and I have seen Johnson walk home—seven blocks—in the rain from his club rather than take a cab, when the same evening he was giving his dinner guests peaches that cost—in December—two dollars and seventy-five cents apiece.

The question is: How far have Johnson's two millions made him a charitable man? I confess that, so far as I can see, giving them up did not cost him the slightest inconvenience. He merely bought a few hundred dollars' worth of reputation—as a charitable millionaire—at a cost of two thousand thousand dollars. It was—commercially—a miserable bargain. Only a comparatively few people of the five million inhabitants of the city of New York ever heard of Johnson or his hospital. Now that it has been built, he is no longer interested. I do not believe he actually got as much satisfaction out of his two-million-dollar investment as he would get out of an evening at the Hippodrome; but who can say that he is not charitable?

* * * * *

I lay stress on this matter of charity because essentially the charitable man is the good man. And by good we mean one who is of value to others as contrasted with one who is working, as most of us are, only for his own pocket all the time. He is the man who is such an egoist that he looks on himself as a part of the whole world and a brother to the rest of mankind. He has really got an exaggerated ego and everybody else profits by it in consequence.

He believes in abstract principles of virtue and would die for them; he recognizes duties and will struggle along, until he is a worn-out, penniless old man, to perform them. He goes out searching for those who need help and takes a chance on their not being deserving. Many a poor chap has died miserably because some rich man has judged that he was not deserving of help. I forget what Lazarus did about the thirsty gentleman in Hades—probably he did not regard him as deserving either.

With most of us a charitable impulse is like the wave made by a stone thrown into a pool—it gets fainter and fainter the farther it has to go. Generally it does not go the length of a city block. It is not enough that there is a starving cripple across the way—he must be on your own doorstep to rouse any interest. When we invest any of our money in charity we want twenty per cent interest, and we want it quarterly. We also wish to have a list of the stockholders made public. A man who habitually smokes two thirty-cent cigars after dinner will drop a quarter into the plate on Sunday and think he is a good Samaritan.

The truth of the matter is that whatever instinct leads us to contribute toward the alleviation of the obvious miseries of the poor should compel us to go further and prevent those miseries—or as many of them as we can—from ever arising at all.

So far as I am concerned, the division of goodness into seven or more specific virtues is purely arbitrary. Virtue is generic. A man is either generous or mean—unselfish or selfish. The unselfish man is the one who is willing to inconvenience or embarrass himself, or to deprive himself of some pleasure or profit for the benefit of others, either now or hereafter.

By the same token, now that I have given thought to the matter, I confess that I am a selfish man—at bottom. Whatever generosity I possess is surface generosity. It would not stand the acid test of self-interest for a moment. I am generous where it is worth my while—that is all; but, like everybody else in my class, I have no generosity so far as my social and business life is concerned. I am willing to inconvenience myself somewhat in my intimate relations with my family or friends, because they are really a part of me—and, anyway, not to do so would result, one way or another, in even greater inconvenience to me.

Once outside my own house, however, I am out for myself and nobody else, however much I may protest that I have all the civic virtues and deceive the public into thinking I have. What would become of me if I did not look out for my own interests in the same way my associates look out for theirs? I should be lost in the shuffle. The Christian virtues may be proclaimed from every pulpit and the Banner of the Cross fly from every housetop; but in business it is the law of evolution and not the Sermon on the Mount that controls.

The rules of the big game are the same as those of the Roman amphitheater. There is not even a pretense that the same code of morals can obtain among corporations and nations as among private individuals. Then why blame the individuals? It is just a question of dog eat dog. We are all after the bone.

No corporation would shorten the working day except by reason of self-interest or legal compulsion. No business man would attack an abuse that would take money out of his own pocket. And no one of us, except out of revenge or pique, would publicly criticize or condemn a man influential enough to do us harm. The political Saint George usually hopes to jump from the back of the dead dragon of municipal corruption into the governor's chair.

We have two standards of conduct—the ostensible and the actual. The first is a convention—largely literary. It is essentially merely a matter of manners—to lubricate the wheels of life. The genuine sphere of its influence extends only to those with whom we have actual contact; so that a breach of it would be embarrassing to us. Within this qualified circle we do business as "Christians & Company, Limited." Outside this circle we make a bluff at idealistic standards, but are guided only by the dictates of self-interest, judged almost entirely by pecuniary tests.

I admit, however, that, though I usually act from selfish motives, I would prefer to act generously if I could do so without financial loss. That is about the extent of my altruism, though I concede an omnipresent consciousness of what is abstractly right and what is wrong. Occasionally, but very rarely, I even blindly follow this instinct irrespective of consequences.

There have been times when I have been genuinely self-sacrificing. Indeed I should unhesitatingly die for my son, my daughters—and probably for my wife. I have frequently suffered financial loss rather than commit perjury or violate my sense of what is right. I have called this sense an instinct, but I do not pretend to know what it is. Neither can I explain its origin. If it is anything it is probably utilitarian; but it does not go very far. I have manners rather than morals.

Fundamentally I am honest, because to be honest is one of the rules of the game I play. If I were caught cheating I should not be allowed to participate. Honesty from this point of view is so obviously the best policy that I have never yet met a big man in business who was crooked. Mind you, they were most of them pirates—frankly flying the black flag and each trying to scuttle the other's ships; but their word was as good as their bond and they played the game squarely, according to the rules. Men of my class would no more stoop to petty dishonesties than they would wear soiled linen. The word lie is not in their mutual language. They may lie to the outside public—I do not deny that they do—but they do not lie to each other.

There has got to be some basis on which they can do business with one another—some stability. The spoils must be divided evenly. Good morals, like good manners, are a necessity in our social relations. They are the uncodified rules of conduct among gentlemen. Being uncodified, they are exceedingly vague; and the court of Public Opinion that administers them is apt to be not altogether impartial. It is a "respecter of persons."

One man can get away with things that another man will hang for. A Jean Valjean will steal a banana and go to the Island, while some rich fellow will put a bank in his pocket and everybody will treat it as a joke. A popular man may get drunk and not be criticized for it; but the sour chap who does the same thing is flung out of the club. There is little justice in the arbitrary decisions of society at large.

In a word we exact a degree of morality from our fellowmen precisely in proportion to its apparent importance to ourselves. It is a purely practical and even a rather shortsighted matter with us. Our friend's private conduct, so far as it does not concern us, is an affair of small moment. He can be as much of a roue as he chooses, so long as he respects our wives and daughters. He can put through a gigantic commercial robbery and we will acclaim his nerve and audacity, provided he is on the level with ourselves. That is the reason why cheating one's club members at cards is regarded as worse than stealing the funds belonging to widows and orphans.

So long as a man conducts himself agreeably in his daily intercourse with his fellows they are not going to put themselves out very greatly to punish him for wrongdoing that does not touch their own bank accounts or which merely violates their private ethical standards. Society is crowded with people who have been guilty of one detestable act, have got thereby on Easy Street and are living happily ever after.

I meet constantly fifteen or twenty men who have deliberately married women for their money—of course without telling them so. According to our professed principles this is—to say the least—obtaining money under false pretenses—a crime under the statutes. These men are now millionaires. They are crooks and swindlers of the meanest sort. Had they not married in this fashion they could not have earned fifteen hundred dollars a year; but everybody goes to their houses and eats their dinners.

There are others, equally numerous, who acquired fortunes by blackmailing corporations or by some deal that at the time of its accomplishment was known to be crooked. To-day they are received on the same terms as men who have been honest all their lives. Society is not particular as to the origin of its food supply. Though we might refuse to steal money ourselves we are not unwilling to let the thief spend it on us. We are too busy and too selfish to bother about trying to punish those who deserve punishment.

On the contrary we are likely to discover surprising virtues in the most unpromising people. There are always extenuating circumstances. Indeed, in those rare instances where, in the case of a rich man, the social chickens come home to roost, the reason his fault is not overlooked is usually so arbitrary or fortuitous that it almost seems an injustice that he should suffer when so many others go scot-free for their misdeeds.

Society has no conscience, and whatever it has as a substitute is usually stimulated only by motives of personal vengeance. It is easier to gloss over an offense than to make ourselves disagreeable and perhaps unpopular.

We have not even the public spirit to have a thief arrested and appear against him in court if he has taken from us only a small amount of money. It is too much trouble. Only when our pride is hurt do we call loudly on justice and honor.

Even revenge is out of fashion. It requires too much effort. Few of us have enough principle to make ourselves uncomfortable in attempting to show disapproval toward wrongdoers. Were this not so, the wicked would not be still flourishing like green bay trees. So long as one steals enough he can easily buy our forgiveness. Honesty is not the best policy—except in trifles.

CHAPTER VI

MY FUTURE

When I began to pen these wandering confessions—or whatever they may properly be called—it was with the rather hazy purpose of endeavoring to ascertain why it was that I, universally conceded to be a successful man, was not happy. As I reread what I have written I realize that, instead of being a successful man in any way, I am an abject failure.

The preceding pages need no comment. The facts speak for themselves. I had everything in my favor at the start. I had youth, health, natural ability, a good wife, friends and opportunity; but I blindly accepted the standards of the men I saw about me and devoted my energies to the achievement of the single object that was theirs—the getting of money.

Thirty years have gone by. I have been a leader in the race and I have secured a prize. But at what cost? I am old—a bundle of undesirable habits; my health is impaired; my wife has become a frivolous and extravagant woman; I have no real friends: my children are strangers to me, and I have no home. I have no interest in my family, my social acquaintances, or in the affairs of the city or nation. I take no sincere pleasure in art or books or outdoor life. The only genuine satisfaction that is mine is in the first fifteen-minutes' flush after my afternoon cocktail and the preliminary course or two of my dinner. I have nothing to look forward to. No matter how much money I make, there is no use to which I can put it that will increase my happiness.

From a material standpoint I have achieved everything I can possibly desire. No king or emperor ever approximated the actual luxury of my daily life. No one ever accomplished more apparent work with less actual personal effort. I am a master at the exploitation of intellectual labor.

I have motors, saddle-horses, and a beautiful summer cottage at a cool and fashionable resort. I travel abroad when the spirit moves me; I entertain lavishly and am entertained in return; I smoke the costliest cigars; I have a reputation at the bar, and I have an established income large enough to sustain at least sixty intelligent people and their families in moderate comfort. This must be true, for on the one hundred and twenty-five dollars a month I pay my chauffeur he supports a wife and two children, sends them to school and on a three-months' vacation into the country during the summer. And, instead of all these things giving me any satisfaction, I am miserable and discontented.

The fact that I now realize the selfishness of my life led me to-day to resolve to do something for others—and this resolve had an unexpected and surprising consequence.

Heretofore I had been engaged in an introspective study of my own attitude toward my fellows. I had not sought the evidence of outside parties. What has just occurred has opened my eyes to the fact that others have not been nearly so blind as I have been myself.

James Hastings, my private secretary, is a man of about forty-five years of age. He has been in my employ fifteen years. He is a fine type of man and deserves the greatest credit for what he has accomplished. Beginning life as an office boy at three dollars a week, he educated himself by attending school at night, learned stenography and typewriting, and has become one of the most expert law stenographers in Wall Street. I believe that, without being a lawyer, he knows almost as much law as I do.

Gradually I have raised his wages until he is now getting fifty dollars a week. In addition to this he does night-work at the Bar Association at double rates, acts as stenographer at legal references, and does, I understand, some trifling literary work besides. I suppose he earns from thirty-five hundred to five thousand dollars a year. About thirteen years ago he married one of the woman stenographers in the office—a nice girl she was too—and now they have a couple of children. He lives somewhere in the country and spends an unconscionable time on the train daily, yet he is always on hand at an early hour.

What happened to-day was this: A peculiarly careful piece of work had been done in the way of looking up a point of corporation law, and I inquired who was responsible for briefing it. Hastings smiled and said he had done so. As I looked at him it suddenly dawned on me that this man might make real money if he studied for the bar and started in practice for himself. He had brains and an enormous capacity for work. I should dislike losing so capable a secretary, but it would be doing him a good turn to let him know what I thought; and it was time that I did somebody a good turn from an unselfish motive.

"Hastings," I said, "you're too good to be merely a stenographer. Why don't you study law and make some money? I'll keep you here in my office, throw things in your way and push you along. What do you say?"

He flushed with gratification, but, after a moment's respectful hesitation, shook his head.

114

"Thank you very much, sir," he replied, "but I wouldn't care to do it. I really wouldn't!"

Though I am fond of the man, his obstinacy nettled me.

"Look here!" I cried. "I'm offering you an unusual chance. You had better think twice before you decline such an opportunity to make something of yourself. If you don't take it you'll probably remain what you are as long as you live. Seize it and you may do as well as I have."

Hastings smiled faintly.

"I'm very sorry, sir," he repeated. "I'm grateful to you for your interest; but—I hope you'll excuse me—I wouldn't change places with you for a million dollars! No—not for ten million!"

He blurted out the last two sentences like a schoolboy, standing and twisting his notebook between his fingers.

There was something in his tone that dashed my spirits like a bucket of cold water. He had not meant to be impertinent. He was the most truthful man alive. What did he mean? Not willing to change places with me! It was my turn to flush.

"Oh, very well!" I answered in as indifferent a manner as I could assume. "It's up to you. I merely meant to do you a good turn. We'll think no more about it."

I continued to think about it, however. Would not change places with me—a fifty-dollar-a-week clerk!

Hastings' pointblank refusal of my good offices, coming as it did hard on the heels of my own realization of failure, left me sick at heart. What sort of an opinion could this honest fellow, my mere employee—dependent on my favor for his very bread—have of me, his master? Clearly not a very high one! I was stung to the quick—chagrined; ashamed.

* * * * *

It was Saturday morning. The week's work was practically over. All of my clients were out of town—golfing, motoring, or playing poker at Cedarhurst. There was nothing for me to do at the office but to indorse half a dozen checks for deposit. I lit a cigar and looked out the window of my cave down on the hurrying throng below. A resolute, never-pausing stream of men plodded in each direction. Now and then others dashed out of the doors of marble buildings and joined the crowd.

On the river ferryboats were darting here and there from shore to shore. There was a bedlam of whistles, the thunder of steam winches, the clang of surface cars, the rattle of typewriters. To what end? Down at the curb my motor car was in waiting. I picked up my hat and passed into the outer office.

"By the way, Hastings," I said casually as I went by his desk, "where are you living now?"

He looked up smilingly.

"Pleasantdale—up Kensico way," he answered.

I shifted my feet and pulled once or twice on my cigar. I had taken a strange resolve.

"Er—going to be in this afternoon?" I asked. "I'm off for a run and I might drop in for a cup of tea about five o'clock."

"Oh, will you, sir!" he exclaimed with pleasure. "We shall be delighted.

Mine is the house at the crossroads—with the red roof."

"Well," said I, "you may see me—but don't keep your tea waiting."

As I shot uptown in my car I had almost the feeling of a coming adventure. Hastings was a good sort! I respected him for his bluntness of speech. At the cigar counter in the club I replenished my case.

Then I went into the reception room, where I found a bunch of acquaintances sitting round the window. They hailed me boisterously. What would I have to drink? I ordered a "Hannah Elias" and sank into a chair. One of them was telling about the newest scandal in the divorce line: The president of one of our largest trust companies had been discovered to have been leading a double life—running an apartment on the West Side for a haggard and passée showgirl.

"You just tell me—I'd like to know—why a fellow like that makes such a damned fool of himself! Salary of fifty thousand dollars a year! Big house; high-class wife and family; yacht— everything anybody wants. Not a drinking man either. It defeats me!" he said.

None of the group seemed able to suggest an answer. I had just tossed off my "Hannah Elias."

"I think I know," I hazarded meditatively. They turned with one accord and stared at me. "There was nothing else for him to do," I continued, "except to blow his brains out."

The raconteur grunted.

"I don't just know the meaning of that!" he remarked. "I thought he was a friend of yours!"

"Oh, I like him well enough," I answered, getting up. "Thanks for the drink. I've got to be getting home. My wife is giving a little luncheon to thirty valuable members of society."

I was delayed on Fifth Avenue and when the butler opened the

116

front door the luncheon party was already seated at the table. A confused din emanated from behind the portières of the dining room, punctuated by shouts of female laughter. The idea of going in and overloading my stomach for an hour, while strenuously attempting to produce light conversation, sickened me. I shook my head.

"Just tell your mistress that I've been suddenly called away on business," I directed the butler and climbed back into my motor.

"Up the river!" I said to my chauffeur.

We spun up the Riverside Drive, past rows of rococo apartment houses, along the Lafayette Boulevard and through Yonkers. It was a glorious autumn day. The Palisades shone red and yellow with turning foliage. There was a fresh breeze down the river and a thousand whitecaps gleamed in the sunlight. Overhead great white clouds moved majestically athwart the blue. But I took no pleasure in it all. I was suffering from an acute mental and physical depression. Like Hamlet I had lost all my mirth—whatever I ever had—and the clouds seemed but a "pestilent congregation of vapors." I sat in a sort of trance as I was whirled farther and farther away from the city.

At last I noticed that my silver motor clock was pointing to half-past two, and I realized that neither the chauffeur nor myself had had anything to eat since breakfast. We were entering a tiny village. Just beyond the main square a sign swinging above the sidewalk invited wayfarers to a "quick lunch." I pressed the button and we pulled to the gravel walk.

"Lunch!" I said, and opened the wire-netted door. Inside there were half a dozen oilcloth-covered tables and a red-cheeked young woman was sewing in a corner.

"What have you got?" I asked, inspecting the layout.

"Tea, coffee, milk—eggs any style you want," she answered cheerily. Then she laughed in a good-natured way. "There's a real hotel at Poughkeepsie—five miles along," she added.

"I don't want a real hotel," I replied. "What are you laughing at?"

Then I realized that I must look rather civilized for a motorist.

"You don't look as you'd care for eggs," she said.

"That's where you're wrong," I retorted. "I want three of the biggest, yellowest, roundest poached eggs your fattest hen ever laid—and a schooner of milk."

The girl vanished into the back of the shop and presently I could smell toast. I discovered I was extremely hungry. In about eight minutes she came back with a tray on which was a large glass

117

of creamy milk and the triple eggs for which I had prayed. They were spherical, white and wabbly.

"You're a prize poacher," I remarked, my spirits reviving.

She smiled appreciatively.

"Going far?" she inquired, sitting down quite at ease at one of the neighboring tables.

I looked pensively at her pleasant face across the eggs.

"That's a question," I answered. "I can't make out whether I've been moving on or just going round and round in a circle."

She looked puzzled for an instant. Then she said shrewdly:

"Perhaps you've really been going back."

"Perhaps," I admitted.

I have never tasted anything quite so good as those eggs and that milk. From where I sat I could look far up the Hudson; the wind from the river swayed the red maples round the door of the quick lunch; and from the kitchen came the homely smells of my lost youth. I had a fleeting vision of the party at my house, now playing bridge for ten cents a point; and my soul lifted its head for the first time in weeks.

"How far is it to Pleasantdale?"

"A long way," answered the girl; "but you can make a connection by trolley that will get you there in about two hours."

"Suits me!" I said and stepped to the door. "You can go, James; I'll get myself home."

He cast on me a scandalized look.

"Very good, sir!" he answered and touched his cap.

He must have thought me either a raving lunatic or an unabashed adventurer. A moment more and the car disappeared in the direction of the city. I was free! The girl made no attempt to conceal her amusement.

Behind the door was a gray felt hat. I took it down and looked at the size. It was within a quarter of my own.

"Look here," I suggested, holding out a five-dollar bill, "I want a Wishing Cap. Let me take this, will you?"

"The house is yours!" she laughed.

Over on the candy counter was a tray of corncob pipes. I helped myself to one, to a package of tobacco and a box of matches. I hung my derby on the vacant peg behind the door. Then I turned to my hostess.

"You're a good girl," I said. "Good luck to you."

For a moment something softer came into her eyes.

"And good luck to you, sir!" she replied. As I passed down the steps she threw after me: "I hope you'll find—what you're looking for!"

* * * * *

In my old felt hat and smoking my corncob I trudged along the road in the mellow sunlight, almost happy. By and by I reached the trolley line; and for five cents, in company with a heterogeneous lot of country folks, Italian laborers and others, was transported an absurdly long distance across the state of New York to a wayside station.

There I sat on a truck on the platform and chatted with a husky, broad-shouldered youth, who said he was the "baggage smasher," until finally a little smoky train appeared and bore me southward. It was the best holiday I had had in years—and I was sorry when we pulled into Pleasantdale and I took to my legs again.

In the fading afternoon light it indeed seemed a pleasant, restful place. Comfortable cottages, each in its own yard, stood in neighborly rows along the shaded street. Small boys were playing football in a field adjoining a schoolhouse.

Presently the buildings became more scattered and I found myself following a real country road, though still less than half a mile from the station. Ahead it divided and in the resulting triangle, behind a well-clipped hedge, stood a pretty cottage with a red roof—Hastings', I was sure.

I tossed away my pipe and opened the gate. A rather pretty woman of about thirty-five was reading in a red hammock; there were half a dozen straw easy chairs and near by a teatable, with the kettle steaming. Mrs. Hastings looked up at my step on the gravel path and smiled a welcome.

"Jim has been playing golf over at the club—he didn't expect you until five," she said, coming to meet me.

"I don't care whether he comes or not," I returned gallantly. "I want to see you. Besides, I'm as hungry as a bear." She raised her eyebrows. "I had only an egg or so and a glass of milk for luncheon, and I have walked—miles!"

"Oh!" she exclaimed. I could see she had had quite a different idea of her erstwhile employer; but my statement seemed to put us on a more friendly footing from the start.

"I love walking too," she hastened to say. "Isn't it wonderful to-day? We get weeks of such weather as this every autumn." She busied herself over the teacups and then, stepping inside the door for a moment, returned with a plate piled high with buttered toast, and another with sandwiches of grape jelly.

"Carmen is out," she remarked; "otherwise you should be served in greater style."

119

"Carmen?"

"Carmen is our maid, butler and valet," she explained. "It's such a relief to get her out of the way once in a while and have the house all to oneself. That's one of the reasons I enjoy our two-weeks' camping trip so much every summer."

"You like the woods?"

"Better than anything, I think—except just being at home here. And the children have the time of their lives—fishing and climbing trees, and watching for deer in the boguns."

The gate clicked at that moment and Hastings, golf bag on shoulders, came up the path. He looked lean, brown, hard and happy.

"Just like me to be late!" he apologized. "I had no idea it would take me so long to beat Colonel Bogey."

"Your excuses are quite unnecessary. Mrs. Hastings and I have discovered that we are natural affinities," said I.

My stenographer, quite at ease, leaned his sticks in a corner and helped himself to a cup of tea and a couple of sandwiches, which in my opinion rivaled my eggs and milk of the early afternoon. My walk had made me comfortably tired; my lungs were distended with cool country air; my head was clear, and this domestic scene warmed the cockles of my heart.

"How is the Chicopee & Shamrock reorganization coming on?" asked Hastings, striving to be polite by suggesting a congenial subject for conversation.

"I don't know," I retorted. "I've forgotten all about it until Monday morning. On the other hand, how are your children coming on?"

"Sylvia is out gathering chestnuts," answered Mrs. Hastings, "and Tom is playing football. They'll be home directly. I wonder if you wouldn't like Jim to show you round our place?"

"Just the thing," I answered, for I guessed she had household duties to perform.

"Of course you'll stay to supper?" she pressed me.

I hesitated, though I knew I should stay, all the time.

"Well—if it really won't put you out," I replied. "I suppose there are evening trains?"

"One every hour. We'll get you home by ten o'clock."

"I'll have to telephone," I said, remembering my wife's regular Saturday-night bridge party.

"That's easily managed," said Hastings. "You can speak to your own house right from my library."

Again I barefacedly excused myself to my butler on the ground of important business. As we strolled through the gateway

120

we were met by a sturdy little boy with tousled hair. He had on an enormous gray sweater and was hugging a pigskin.

"We beat 'em!" he shouted, unabashed by my obviously friendly presence.

"Eighteen to nothing!"

"Tom is twelve," said Hastings with a shade of pride in his voice. "Yes, the schools here are good. I expect to have him ready for college in five years more."

"What are you going to make of him?" I asked.

"A civil engineer, I think," he answered. "You see, I'm a crank on fresh air and building things—and he seems to be like me. This cooped-up city life is pretty narrowing, don't you think?"

"It's fierce!" I returned heartily, with more warmth than elegance.

"Sometimes I wish I could chuck the whole business and go to farming."

"Why not?" he asked as we climbed a small rise behind the house. "Here's my farm—fifteen acres. We raise most of our own truck."

Below the hill a cornfield, now yellow with pumpkins, stretched to the farther road. Nearer the house was a kitchen garden, with an apple orchard beyond. A man in shirtsleeves was milking a cow behind a tiny barn.

"I bought this place three years ago for thirty-nine hundred dollars," said my stenographer. "They say it is worth nearer six thousand now. Anyhow it is worth a hundred thousand to me!"

A little girl, with bulging apron, appeared at the edge of the orchard and came running toward us.

"What have you got there?" called her father.

"Oh, daddy! Such lovely chestnuts!" cried the child. "And there are millions more of them!"

"We'll roast 'em after supper," said her father. "Toddle along now and wash up."

She put up a rosy, beaming face to be kissed and dashed away toward the house. I tried to remember what either of my two girls had been like at her age, but for some strange reason I could not.

Across the road the fertile countryside sloped away into a distant valley, hemmed in by dim blue hills, below which the sun had already sunk, leaving only a gilded edge behind. The air was filled with a soft, smoky haze. A church bell in the village struck six o'clock.

"The curfew tolls the knell of parting day,
The lowing herd winds slowly o'er the lea,

121

The plowman homeward plods his weary way,"

I murmured.

"For 'plowman' read 'golfer,'" smiled my host. "By George, though—it is pretty good to be alive!" The air had turned crisp and we both instinctively took a couple of deep breaths. "Makes the city look like thirty cents!" he ejaculated. "Of course it isn't like New York or Southampton."

"No, thank God! It isn't!" I muttered as we wandered toward the house.

"I hope you don't mind an early supper," apologized Mrs. Hastings as we entered; "but Jim gets absolutely ravenous. You see, on weekdays his lunch is at best a movable feast."

Our promptly served meal consisted of soup, scrambled eggs and bacon, broiled chops, fried potatoes, peas, salad, apple pie, cheese, grapes plucked fresh from the garden wall, and black coffee, distilled from a shining coffee machine. Mrs. Hastings brought the things hot from the kitchen and dished them herself. Tom and Sylvia, carefully spruced up, ate prodigiously and then helped clear away the dishes, while I produced my cigar case.

Then Hastings led me across the hall to a room about twelve feet square, the walls of which were lined with books, where a wood fire was already crackling cozily. Motioning me to an old leather armchair, he pulled up a wooden rocker before the mantel and, leaning over, laid a regiment of chestnuts before the blazing logs.

I stretched out my legs and took a long pull on one of my Carona-Caronas. It all seemed too good to be true. Only six hours before in my marble entrance hall I had listened disgustedly to the cackle of my wife's luncheon party behind the tapestry of my own dining room.

After all, how easy it was to be happy! Here was Hastings, jolly as a clam and living like a prince on—what? I wondered.

"Hastings," I said, "do you mind telling me how much it costs you to live like this?"

"Not at all," he replied—"though I never figured it out exactly. Let's see. Five per cent on the cost of the place—say, two hundred dollars. Repairs and insurance a hundred. That's three hundred, isn't it? We pay the hired man thirty-five dollars and Carmen eighteen dollars a month, and give 'em their board—about six hundred and fifty more. So far nine hundred and fifty. Our vegetables and milk cost us practically nothing—meat and groceries about seventy-five a month—nine hundred a year.

"We have one horse; but in good weather I use my bicycle to go to the station. We cut our own ice in the pond back of the

122

orchard. The schools are free. I cut quite a lot of wood myself, but my coal comes high—must cost me at least a hundred and fifty a year. I don't have many doctors' bills, living out here; but the dentist hits us for about twenty-five dollars every six months—that's fifty more. My wife spends about three hundred and the children as much more. Of course that's fairly liberal. One doesn't need ballgowns in our village.

"My own expenses are, railroad fare, lunches, tobacco—I smoke a pipe mostly—and clothes—probably about five hundred in all. We go on a big bat once a month and dine at a table-d'hôte restaurant, and take in the opera or the play. That costs some— about ten dollars a clip—say, eighty for the season; and, of course, I blow the kids to a camping trip every summer, which sets me back a good hundred and fifty. How does that come out?"

I had jotted the items down, as he went along, on the back of an envelope.

"Thirty-three hundred and eighty dollars," I said, adding them up.

"It seems a good deal," he commented, turning and gazing into the fire; "but I have usually managed to lay up about fifteen hundred every year—besides, of course, the little I give away."

I sat stunned. Thirty-three hundred dollars!—I spent seventy-two thousand!—and the man lived as well as I did! What did I have that he had not? But Hastings was saying something, still with his back toward me.

"I suppose you thought I must be an ungrateful dog not to jump at the offer you made me this morning," he remarked in an embarrassed manner. "It's worried me a lot all day. I'm really tremendously gratified at your kindness. I couldn't very well explain myself, and I don't know what possessed me to say what I did about my not being willing to exchange places with you. But, you see, I'm over forty. That makes a heap of difference. I'm as good a stenographer as you can find, and so long as my health holds out I can be sure of at least fifty dollars a week, besides what I earn outside.

"I've never had any kink for the law. I don't think I'd be a success at it; and frankly, saving your presence, I don't like it. A lot of it is easy money and a lot of it is money earned in the meanest way there is—playing dirty tricks; putting in the wrong a fellow that's really right; aggravating misunderstandings and profiting by the quarrels people get into. You're a high-class, honorable man, and you don't see the things I see." I winced. If he only knew, I had seen a good deal! "But I go round among the other law offices, and I tell you it's a demoralizing profession.

123

"It's all right to reorganize a railroad; but in general litigation it seems to me as if the lawyers spend most of their time trying to make the judge and jury believe the witnesses are all criminals. Everything a man says on the stand or has ever done in his life is made the subject of a false inference—an innuendo. The law isn't constructive—it's destructive; and that's why I want my boy to be a civil engineer."

He paused, abashed at his own heat.

"Well," I interjected, "it's a harsh arraignment; but there's a great deal of truth in what you say. Wouldn't you like to make big money?"

"Big money! I do make big money—for a man of my class," he replied with a gentle smile. "I wouldn't know what to do with much more. I've got health and a comfortable home, the affection of an honest woman and two fine children. I work hard, sleep like a log, and get a couple of sets of tennis or a round of golf on Saturdays and Sundays. I have the satisfaction of knowing I give you your money's worth for the salary you pay me. My kids have as good teachers as there are anywhere. We see plenty of people and I belong to a club or two. I bear a good reputation in the town and try to keep things going in the right direction. We have all the books and magazines we want to read. What's more, I don't worry about trying to be something I'm not."

"How do you mean?" I asked, feeling that his talk was money in my moral pocket.

"Oh, I've seen a heap of misery in New York due to just wanting to get ahead—I don't know where; fellows that are just crazy to make 'big money' as you call it, in order to ride in motors and get into some sort of society. All the clerks, office boys and stenographers seem to want to become stockbrokers. Personally I don't see what there is in it for them. I don't figure out that my boy would be any happier with two million dollars than without. If he had it he would be worrying all the time for fear he wasn't getting enough fun for his money. And as for my girl I want her to learn to do something! I want her to have the discipline that comes from knowing how to earn her own living. Of course that's one of the greatest satisfactions there is in life anyway—doing some one thing as well as it can be done."

"Wouldn't you like your daughter to marry?" I demanded.

"Certainly—if she can find a clean man who wants her. Why, it goes without saying, that is life's greatest happiness—that and having children."

"Certainly!" I echoed with an inward qualm.

"Suppose she doesn't marry though? That's the point. She

124

doesn't want to hang round a boarding house all her life when everybody is busy doing interesting things. I've got a theory that the reason rich people—especially rich women—get bored is because they don't know anything about real life. Put one of 'em in a law office, hitting a typewriter at fifteen dollars a week, and in a month she'd wake up to what was really going on—she'd be alive!"

"'The world is so full of a number of things I'm sure we should all be as happy as kings!'"

said I. "What's Sylvia going to do?"

"Oh, she's quite a clever little artist." He handed me some charming sketches in pencil that were lying on the table. "I think she may make an illustrator. Heaven knows we need 'em! I'll give her a course at Pratt Institute and then at the Academy of Design; and after that, if they think she is good enough, I'll send her to Paris."

"I wish I'd done the same thing with my girls!" I sighed. "But the trouble is—the trouble is—You see, if I had they wouldn't have been doing what their friends were doing. They'd have been out of it."

"No; they wouldn't like that, of course," agreed Hastings respectfully.

"They would want to be 'in it'"

I looked at him quickly to see whether his remark had a double entendre.

"I don't see very much of my daughters," I continued. "They've got away from me somehow."

"That's the tough part of it," he said thoughtfully. "I suppose rich people are so busy with all the things they have to do that they haven't much time for fooling round with their children. I have a good time with mine though. They're too young to get away anyhow. We read French history aloud every evening after supper. Sylvia is almost an expert on the Duke of Guise and the Massacre of St. Bartholomew."

We smoked silently for some moments. Hastings' ideas interested me, but I felt that he could give me something more personal—of more value to myself. The fellow was really a philosopher in his quiet way.

"After all, you haven't told me what you meant by saying you wouldn't change places with me," I said abruptly. "What did you mean by that? I want to know."

"I wish you would forget I ever said it, sir," he murmured.

"No," I retorted, "I can't forget it. You needn't spare me. This

125

talk is not ex cathedra—it's just between ourselves. When you've told me why, then I will forget it. This is man to man."

"Well," he answered slowly, "it would take me a long time to put it in just the right way. There was nothing personal in what I said this morning. I was thinking about conditions in general—the whole thing. It can't go on!"

"What can't go on?"

"The terrible burden of money," he said.

"Terrible burden of money!" I repeated. What did he mean?

"The weight of it—that's bowing people down and choking them up. It's like a ball and chain. I meant I wouldn't change places with any man in the millionaire class—I couldn't stand the complexities and responsibilities. I believe the time is coming when no citizen will be permitted to receive an income from his inherited or accumulated possessions greater than is good for him. You may say that's the wildest sort of socialism. Perhaps it is. But it's socialism looked at from a different angle from the platform orators—the angle of the individual.

"I don't believe a man's money should be taken away from him and distributed round for the sake of other people—but for the protection of the man himself. There's got to be a pecuniary safety valve. Every dollar over a certain amount, just like every extra pound of steam in a boiler, is a thing of danger. We want health in the individual and in the state—not disease.

"Let the amount of a man's income be five, ten, fifteen or twenty thousand dollars—the exact figure doesn't matter; but there is a limit at which wealth becomes a drag and a detriment instead of a benefit! I'd base the legality of a confiscatory income tax on the constitutionality of any health regulation or police ordinance. People shouldn't be permitted to injure themselves—or have poison lying round. Certainly it's a lesson that history teaches on every page.

"Besides everybody needs something to work for—to keep him fit—at least that's the way it looks to me. Nations—let alone mere individuals—have simply gone to seed, died of dry rot because they no longer had any stimulus. A fellow has got to have some idea in the back of his head as to what he's after—and the harder it is for him to get it, the better, as a rule, it is for him. Good luck is the worst enemy a heap of people have. Misfortune spurs a man on, tries him out and develops him—makes him more human."

"Ever played in hard luck?" I queried.

"I? Sure, I have," answered Hastings cheerfully. "And I wouldn't worry much if it came my way again. I could manage to get along pretty comfortably on less than half I've got. I like my home;

126

but we could be happy anywhere so long as we had ourselves and our health and a few books. However, I wasn't thinking of myself. I've got a friend in the brokering business who says it's the millionaires that do most of the worrying anyhow. Naturally a man with a pile of money has to look after it; but what puzzles me is why anybody should want it in the first place."

He searched along a well-filled and disordered shelf of shabby books.

"Here's what William James says about it:

"'We have grown literally afraid to be poor. We despise any one who elects to be poor in order to simplify and save his inner life. We have lost the power of even imagining what the ancient idealization of poverty could have meant—the liberation from material attachments; the unbribed soul; the manlier indifference; the paying our way by what we are or do, and not by what we have; the right to fling away our life at any moment irresponsibly—the more athletic trim, in short the moral fighting shape.... It is certain that the prevalent fear of poverty among the educated class is the worst moral disease from which our civilization suffers.'"

"I guess he's about right," I agreed.

"That's my idea exactly," answered Hastings. "As I look at it the curse of most of the people living on Fifth Avenue is that they're perfectly safe. You could take away nine-tenths of what they've got and they'd still have about a hundred times more money than they needed to be comfortable. They're like a whole lot of fat animals in an inclosure—they're fed three or four times a day, but the wire fence that protects them from harm deprives them of any real liberty. Or they're like goldfish swimming round and round in a big bowl. They can look through sort of dimly; but they can't get out! If they really knew, they'd trade their security for their freedom any time.

"Perfect safety isn't an unmixed blessing by any means. Look at the photographs of the wild Indians—the ones that carried their lives in their hands every minute—and there's something stern and noble about their faces. Put an Indian on a reservation and he takes to drinking whisky. It was the same way with the chaps that lived in the Middle Ages and had to wear shirts of chainmail. It kept 'em guessing. That's merely one phase of it.

"The real thing to put the bite into life is having a Cause. People forget how to make sacrifices—or become afraid to. After all, even dying isn't such a tremendous trick. Plenty of people have done it just for an idea—wanted to pray in their own way. But this modern way of living takes all the sap out of folks. They get an entirely false impression of the relative values of things. It takes a failure or a death in the family to wake them up to the comparative triviality of the worth of money as compared, for instance, to human affection—any of the real things of life.

"I don't object to inequality of mere wealth in itself, because I wouldn't dignify money to that extent. Of course I do object to a situation where the rich man can buy life and health for his sick child and the poor man can't. Too many sick babies! That'll be attended to, all right, in time. I wouldn't take away one man's money for the sake of giving it to others—not a bit of it. But what I would do would be to put it out of a man's power to poison himself with money.

"Suicide is made a crime under the law. How about moral and intellectual suicide? It ought to be prevented for the sake of the state. No citizen should be allowed to stultify himself with luxury any more than he should be permitted to cut off his right hand. Excuse me for being didactic—but you said you'd like to get my point of view and I've tried to give it to you in a disjointed sort of way. I'd sooner my son would have to work for his living than not, and I'd rather he'd spend his life contending with the forces of nature and developing the country than in quarreling over the division of profits that other men had earned."

I had listened attentively to what Hastings had to say; and, though I did not agree with all of it, I was forced to admit the truth of a large part. He certainly seemed to have come nearer to solving the problem than I had even been able to. Yet it appeared to my conservative mind shockingly socialistic and chimerical.

"So you really think," I retorted, "that the state ought to pass laws which should prevent the accumulation—or at least the retention—of large fortunes?"

Hastings smiled apologetically.

"Well," he answered, "I don't know just how far I should advocate active governmental interference, though it's a serious question. You're a thousand times better qualified to express an opinion on that than I am.

"When I spoke about health and police regulations I was talking metaphorically. I suppose my real idea is that the moral force of the community—public opinion—ought to be strong enough to compel a man to live so that such laws would be unnecessary. His own public spirit, his conscience, or whatever you call it, should influence him to use whatever he has above a certain amount for the common good—to turn it back where he got it, or somebody else got it, instead of demoralizing the whole country and setting an example of waste and extravagance. That kind of thing does an awful lot of harm. I see it all round me. But, of course, the worst

128

sufferer is the man himself, and his own good sense ought to jack him up.

"Still you can't force people to keep healthy. If a man is bound to sacrifice everything for money and make himself sick with it, perhaps he ought to be prevented."

"Jim!" cried Mrs. Hastings, coming in with a pitcher of cider and some glasses. "I could hear you talking all the way out in the kitchen. I'm sure you've bored our guest to death. Why, the chestnuts are burned to a crisp!"

"He hasn't bored me a bit," I answered; "in fact we are agreed on a great many things. However, after I've had a glass of that cider I must start back to town."

"We'd love to have you spend the night," she urged. "We've a nice little guestroom over the library."

The invitation was tempting, but I wanted to get away and think. Also it was my duty to look in on the bridge party before it became too sleepy to recognize my presence. I drank my cider, bade my hostess good night and walked to the station with Hastings. As we crossed the square to the train he said:

"It was mighty good of you to come out here to see us and we both appreciate it. Hope you'll forgive my bluntness this morning and for shooting off my mouth so much this evening."

"My dear fellow," I returned, "that was what I came out for. You've given me something to think about. I'm thinking already. You're quite right. You'd be a fool to change places with anybody— let alone a miserable millionaire."

* * * * *

In the smoker of the accommodation, to which I retired, I sat oblivious of my surroundings until we entered the tunnel. So far as I could see, Hastings had it on me at every turn—at thirty-three hundred a year—considerably less than half of what I paid out annually in servants' wages. And the exasperating part of it all was that, though I spent seventy-two thousand a year, I did not begin to be as happy as he was! Not by a jugful. Face to face with the simple comfort of the cottage I had just left, its sincerity and affection, its thrifty self-respect, its wide interests, I confessed that I had not been myself genuinely contented since I left my mother's house for college, thirty odd years before. I had become the willing victim of a materialistic society.

I had squandered my life in a vain effort to purchase happiness with money—an utter impossibility, as I now only too plainly saw. I was poisoned with it, as Hastings had said—sick with it and sick of it. I was one of Hastings' chaingangs of prosperous prisoners—millionaires shackled together and walking in lockstep; one of his school of goldfish bumping their noses against the glass of the bowl in which they were confined by virtue of their inability to live outside the medium to which they were accustomed.

I was through with it! From that moment I resolved to become a free man; living my own life; finding happiness in things that were worth while. I would chuck the whole nauseating business of valets and scented baths; of cocktails, clubs and cards; of an unwieldy and tiresome household of lazy servants; of the ennui of heavy dinners; and of a family the members of which were strangers to each other. I could and would easily cut down my expenditures to not more than thirty thousand a year; and with the balance of my income I would look after some of those sick babies Hastings had mentioned.

I would begin by taking a much smaller house and letting half the servants go, including my French cook. I had for a long time realized that we all ate too much. I would give up one of my motors and entertain more simply. We would omit the spring dash to Paris, and I would insist on a certain number of evenings each week which the family should spend together, reading aloud or talking over their various plans and interests. It did not seem by any means impossible in the prospect and I got a considerable amount of satisfaction from planning it all out. My life was to be that of a sort of glorified Hastings. After my healthy, peaceful day in the quiet country I felt quite light-hearted—as nearly happy as I could remember having been for years.

It was raining when I got out at the Grand Central Station, and as I hurried along the platform to get a taxi I overtook an acquaintance of mine—a social climber. He gave me a queer look in response to my greeting and I remembered that I had on the old gray hat I had taken from the quick lunch.

"I've been off for a tramp in the country," I explained, resenting my own instinctive embarrassment.

"Ah! Don't say! Didn't know you went in for that sort of thing! Well, good night!"

He sprang into the only remaining taxi without asking me to share it and vanished in a cloud of gasoline smoke. I was in no mood for waiting; besides I was going to be democratic. I took a surface car up Lexington Avenue and stood between the distended knees of a fat and somnolent Italian gentleman for thirty blocks. The car was intolerably stuffy and smelled strongly of wet umbrellas and garlic. By the time I reached the cross-street on which I lived it had begun to pour. I turned up my coat collar and ran to my house.

Somehow I felt like a small boy as I threw myself panting inside my own marble portal. My butler expressed great sympathy for my condition and smuggled me quickly upstairs. I fancy he suspected there was something discreditable about my absence. A pungent aroma floated up from the drawing room, where the bridge players were steadily at work. I confess to feeling rather dirty, wet and disreputable.

"I'm sorry, sir," said my butler as he turned on the electric switch in my bedroom, "but I didn't expect you back this evening, and so I told Martin he might go out."

A wave of irritation, almost of anger, swept over me. Martin was my perfect valet.

"What the devil did you do that for!" I snapped.

Then, realizing my inconsistency, I was ashamed, utterly humiliated and disgusted with myself. This, then, was all that my resolution amounted to after all!

"I am very sorry, sir," repeated my butler. "Very sorry, sir, indeed. Shall I help you off with your things?"

"Oh, that's all right!" I exclaimed, somewhat to his surprise. "Don't bother about me. I'll take care of myself."

"Can't I bring you something?" he asked solicitously.

"No, thanks!" said I. "I don't need anything that you can give me!"

"Very good, sir," he replied. "Good night, sir."

"Good night," I answered, and he closed the door noiselessly.

I lit a cigarette and, tossing off my coat, sank into a chair. My mere return to that ordered elegance seemed to have benumbed my individuality. Downstairs thirty of our most intimate friends were amusing themselves at the cardtables, confident that at eleven-thirty they would be served with supper consisting of salads, ice-cream and champagne. They would not hope in vain. If they did not get it—speaking broadly—they would not come again. They wanted us as we were—house, food, trappings—the whole layout. They meant well enough. They simply had to have certain things. If we changed our scale of living we should lose the acquaintance of these people, and we should have nobody in their place.

We had grown into a highly complicated system, in which we had a settled orbit. This orbit was not susceptible of change unless we were willing to turn everything topsy-turvy. Everybody would suppose we had lost our money. And, not being brilliant or clever people, who paid their way as they went by making themselves lively and attractive, it would be assumed that we could not keep up our end; so we should be gradually left out.

I said to myself that I ought not to care—that being left out

131

was what I wanted; but, all the same, I knew I did care. You cannot tear yourself up by the roots at fifty unless you are prepared to go to a far country. I was not prepared to do that at a moment's notice. I, too, was used to a whole lot of things—was solidly imbedded in them.

My very house was an overwhelming incubus. I was like a miserable snail, forever lugging my house round on my back— unable to shake it off. A change in our mode of life would not necessarily in itself bring my children any nearer to me; it would, on the contrary, probably antagonize them. I had sowed the seed and I was reaping the harvest. My professional life I could not alter. I had my private clients—my regular business. Besides there was no reason for altering it. I conducted it honorably and well enough.

Yet the calm consideration of those very difficulties in the end only demonstrated the clearer to me the perilous state in which I was. The deeper the bog, the more my spirit writhed to be free. Better, I thought, to die struggling than gradually to sink down and be suffocated beneath the mire of apathy and self-indulgence.

Hastings' little home—or something—had wrought a change in me. I had gone through some sort of genuine emotional experience. It seemed impossible to reform my mode of life and thought, but it was equally incredible that I should fall back into my old indifference. Sitting there alone in my chamber I felt like a man in a nightmare, who would give his all to be able to rise, yet whose limbs were immovable, held by some subtle and cruel power. I had read in novels about men agonized by remorse and indecision. I now experienced those sensations myself. I discovered they were not imaginary states.

My meditations were interrupted by the entrance of my wife, who, with an anxious look on her face, inquired what was the matter. The butler had said I seemed indisposed; so she had slipped away from our guests and come up to see for herself. She was in full regalia—elaborate gown, pearls, aigret.

"There's nothing the matter with me," I answered, though I know full well I lied—I was poisoned.

"Well, that's a comfort, at any rate!" she replied, amiably enough.

"Where's Tom?" I asked wearily.

"I haven't any idea," she said frankly. "You know he almost never comes home."

"And the girls?"

"Visiting the Devereuxs at Staatsburg," she answered. "Aren't you coming down for some bridge?"

"No," I said. "To tell you the truth I never want to see a pack of

132

cards again. I want to cut the game. I'm sick of our life and the useless extravagance. I want a change. Let's get rid of the whole thing—take a smaller house—have fewer servants. Think of the relief!"

"What's the matter?" she cried sharply. "Have you lost money?"

Money! Money!

"No," I said, "I haven't lost money—I've lost heart!"

She eyed me distrustfully.

"Are you crazy?" she demanded.

"No," I answered. "I don't think I am."

"You act that way," she retorted. "It's a funny time to talk about changing your mode of life—right in the middle of a bridge party! What have you been working for all these years? And where do I come in? You can go to your clubs and your office—anywhere; but all I've got is the life you have taught me to enjoy! Tom is grown up and never comes near me. And the girls—why, what do you think would happen to them if you suddenly gave up your place in society? They'd never get married so long as they lived. People would think you'd gone bankrupt! Really"—her eyes filled and she dabbed at them with a Valenciennes handkerchief—"I think it too heartless of you to come in this way—like a skeleton at the feast— and spoil my evening!"

I felt a slight touch of remorse. I had broached the matter rather roughly. I laid my hand on her shoulder—now so round and matronly, once so slender.

"Anna," I said as tenderly as I could, "suppose I did give it all up?"

She rose indignantly to her feet and shook off my hand.

"You'd have to get along without me!" she retorted; then, seeing the anguish on my face, she added less harshly: "Take a brandy-and-soda and go to bed. I'm sure you're not quite yourself."

I was struck by the chance significance of her phrase—"Not quite yourself." No; ever since I had left the house that morning I had not been quite myself. I had had a momentary glimpse—had for an instant caught the glint of an angel's wing—but it was gone. I was almost myself—my old self; yet not quite.

"I didn't mean to be unkind," I muttered. "Don't worry about me. I've merely had a vision of what might have been, and it's disgusted me. Go on down to the bridge fiends. I'll be along shortly—if you'll excuse my clothes."

"Poor boy!" she sighed. "You're tired out! No; don't come down—in those clothes!"

133

I laughed a hollow laugh when she had gone. Really there was something humorous about it all. What was the use even of trying? I did not seem even to belong in my own house unless my clothes matched the wall paper! I lit cigarette after cigarette, staring blankly at my silk pajamas laid out on the bed.

I could not change things! It was too late. I had brought up my son and daughters to live in a certain kind of way, had taught them that luxuries were necessities, had neglected them—had ruined them perhaps; but I had no moral right now to annihilate that life— and their mother's—without their consent. They might be poor things; but, after all, they were my own. They were free, white and twenty-one. And I knew they would simply think me mad!

I had a fixed place in a complicated system, with responsibilities and duties I was morally bound to recognize. I could not chuck the whole business without doing a great deal of harm. My life was not so simple as all that. Any change—if it could be accomplished at all—would have to be a gradual one and be brought about largely by persuasion. Could it be accomplished?

It now seemed insuperably difficult. I was bound to the wheel—and the habits of a lifetime, the moral pressure of my wife and children, the example of society, and the force of superficial public opinion and expectation were spinning it round and round in the direction of least resistance. As well attempt to alter my course as to steer a locomotive off the track! I could not ditch the locomotive, for I had a trainload of passengers! And yet—

I groaned and buried my face in my hands. I—successful? Yes, success had been mine; but success was failure—naught else— failure, absolute and unmitigated! I had lost my wife and family, and my home had become the resort of a crew of empty-headed coxcombs.

I wondered whether they were gone. I looked at the clock. It was half-past twelve—Sunday morning. I opened my bedroom door and crept downstairs. No; they were not gone—they had merely moved on to supper.

My library was in the front of the house, across the hall from the drawing room, and I went in there and sank into an armchair by the fire. The bridge party was making a great to-do and its strident laughter floated up from below. By contrast the quiet library seemed a haven of refuge. Here were the books I might have read—which might have been my friends. Poor fool that I was!

I put out my hand and took down the first it encountered—

John Bunyan's Pilgrim's Progress. It was a funny old volume—a priceless early edition given me by a grateful client whom I had extricated from some embarrassment. I had never read it, but I knew its general trend. It was about some imaginary miserable who, like myself, wanted to do things differently. I took a cigar out of my pocket, lit it and, opening the book haphazard, glanced over the pages in a desultory fashion.

"That is that which I seek for, even to be rid of this heavy Burden; but get it off myself, I cannot; nor is there any man in our country that can take it off my shoulders—"

So the Pilgrim had a burden too! I turned back to the beginning and read how Christian, the hero, had been made aware of his perilous condition.

"In this plight therefore he went home, and refrained himself as long as he could, that his Wife and Children should not perceive his distress, but he could not be silent long, because that his trouble increased: Wherefore at length he brake his mind to his Wife and Children; and thus he began to talk to them: 'Oh, my dear Wife,' said he, 'and you the Children of my bowels, I, your dear Friend, am in myself undone by reason of a Burden that lieth hard upon me.' ... At this his Relations were sore amazed; not for that they believed that what he had said to them was true, but because they thought that some frenzy distemper had got into his head; therefore, it drawing toward night, and they hoping that sleep might settle his brains, with all haste they got him to bed: But the night was as troublesome to him as the day; wherefore, instead of sleeping, he spent it in sighs and tears."

Surely this Pilgrim was strangely like myself! And, though sorely beset, he had struggled on his way.

"Hast thou a Wife and Children?

"Yes, but I am so laden with this Burden that I cannot take that pleasure in them as formerly; methinks I am as if I had none."

Tears filled my eyes and I laid down the book. The bridge party was going home. I could hear them shouting good-bys in the front hall and my wife's shrill voice answering Good night! From outside came the toot of horns and the whir of the motors as they drew up at the curb. One by one the doors slammed, the glass rattled and they thundered off. The noise got on my nerves and, taking my book, I crossed to the deserted drawing room, the scene of the night's social carnage. The sight was enough to sicken any man! Eight tables covered with half-filled glasses; cards everywhere—the floor littered with them; chairs pushed helter-skelter and one overturned; and from a dozen ash-receivers the slowly ascending columns of incense to the great God of Chance. On the middle table lay a score card and pencil, a roll of bills, a pile of silver, and my wife's vanity box, with its chain of pearls and diamonds.

Fiercely I resolved again to end it all—at any cost. I threw open one of the windows, sat myself down by a lamp in a corner, and found the place where I had been reading. Christian had just encountered Charity. In the midst of their discussion I heard my wife's footsteps in the hall; the portières rustled and she entered.

"Well!" she exclaimed. "I thought you had gone to bed long ago. I had good luck to-night. I won eight hundred dollars! How are you feeling?"

"Anna," I answered, "sit down a minute. I want to read you something."

"Go ahead!" she said, lighting a cigarette, and throwing herself into one of the vacant chairs.

"Then said Charity to Christian: Have you a family? Are you a married man?"

"CHRISTIAN: I have a Wife and ... Children."

"CHARITY: And why did you not bring them along with you?"

"Then Christian wept and said: Oh, how willingly would I have done it, but they were all of them utterly averse to my going on Pilgrimage."

"CHARITY: But you should have talked to them, and have endeavored to have shown them the danger of being behind.

"CHRISTIAN: So I did, and told them also what God had shewed to me of the destruction of our City; but I seemed to them as one that mocked, and they believed me not.

"CHARITY: And did you pray to God that He would bless your counsel to them?

"CHRISTIAN: Yes, and that with much affection; for you must think that my Wife and poor Children were very dear unto me.

"CHARITY: But did you tell them of your own sorrow and fear of destruction?—for I suppose that destruction was visible enough to you.

"CHRISTIAN: Yes, over and over, and over. They might also see my fears in my countenance, in my tears, and also in my trembling under the apprehension of the Judgment that did hang over our heads; but all was not sufficient to prevail with them to come with me.

"CHARITY: But what could they say for themselves, why they come not?

"CHRISTIAN: Why, my Wife was afraid of losing this World, and my Children were given to the foolish Delights of youth; so,

136

what by one thing and what by another, they left me to wander in this manner alone."

An unusual sound made me look up. My wife was weeping, her head on her arms among the money and débris of the card-table.

"I—I didn't know," she said in a choked, half-stifled voice, "that you really meant what you said upstairs."

"I mean it as I never have meant anything since I told you that I loved you, dear," I answered gently.

She raised her face, wet with tears.

"That was such a long time ago!" she sobbed. "And I thought that all this was what you wanted." She glanced round the room.

"I did—once," I replied; "but I don't want it any longer. We can't live our lives over again; but"—and I went over to her—"we can try to do a little better from now on."

She laid her head on my arm and took my hand in hers.

"What shall we do?" she asked.

"We must free ourselves from our Burden," said I; "break down the wall of money that shuts us in from other people, and try to pay our way in the world by what we are and do rather than by what we have. It may be hard at first; but it's worth while—for all of us."

She disengaged one hand and wiped her eyes.

"I'll help all I can," she whispered.

"That's what I want!" cried I, and my heart leaped.

Again I saw the glint of the angel's wing!

www.ingramcontent.com/pod-product-compliance
Lightning Source LLC
Chambersburg PA
CBHW011514170626
46810CB00009B/3357